FORTY ACRES DEEP

FORTY ACRES DEEP

Michael Perry

For Sturgill Simpson.
He don't need me but I sure needed him.

Chapter One

Harold had come to consider the accumulating weight of snow on the farmhouse roof as his life's unfinished business. Daily the load grew…on his heart, his head, the creaking eaves.

There had been no blizzard. The flakes had fallen through stillness and hush. Inch after inch, then foot after foot. With no wind to whip or drift it, the snow simply settled, forming marshmallow abstractions of whatever lay beneath. He thumbed a peephole in the window frost; every pine tree was capped, every outbuilding banked. The bulldozer beside the machine shed looked as if it were coiffed in meringue. Only the oaks broke the motif, their bare branches arrayed as fossilized veins against the sky.

She died a month ago, and he hadn't plowed the driveway since. In the old days someone would have showed up by now. Noticed the lack of tracks, waded through the drifts to knock on the door. Waited just long enough not to be nosy, checked in just soon enough to be neighborly.

The old days. He had come to despise the phrase. Three words, like hard candy gone rancid on the tongue. The taste of futile yearning. A cold soup of curdled memories. A toothless whine. As a child he loved listening as the old-timers shot dice around the coffee pot down at Peterson's Implement. Thirty years later, after all the farm bankruptcies finally pulled Peterson's under, the new generation of oldsters stood in a sad huddle at the auction, nursing convenience store cappuccinos and shaking their heads at *things these days*. Harold bid five dollars for a set of old wrenches, paid at the cashier's trailer, and on the drive home swore he wouldn't die trying to claw the past into the present.

That morning in the bed he checked for a pulse but knew immediately by the coolness of her wrist. He'd volunteered with the local fire and rescue for years, so he knew to turn her, check for lividity. It had been some hours.

He wrapped her in blankets and placed her on the porch. All day the house was silent, save the snap of the fire, the click in his ankle, the stewpot bubbling.

He had no idea what to do.

He knew he did not want help.

It was snowing again.

The ground had lain bare well into November. The landscape bleak, brown and hard. Mornings when he watered the beef cattle, he'd bust the ice with a hatchet. The shards skittered across the frozen mud, every lump an unforgiving nub. He found himself hoping for snow. Anything to soften the landscape.

At Christmas there had been flurries. At New Year's, a light half-inch. Took her half a minute to sweep it from the steps. Same with the sidewalk. Didn't even bother fetching the shovel. Three weeks later there was snow to the window boxes. He imagined her final breath resting as frost against the glass.

He still thought of himself as a farmer. In fact he hadn't milked a cow since the barn burned. The insurance company paid to have the whole smoldering works shoved into a hole. That was hell to watch. On heavy, fogged-in days he swore he could smell it still: burnt wires, burnt hay, burnt hooves, burnt beef. A decade gone, and still the recollection of lurching awake to bawling cattle and a shuddering orange glow out the bedroom window surged in his throat. Dairying had always been an act of love and desperation, but even after most of his neighbors bit the dust, he had hung in. The blaze and the bankers ended that. He switched to beef cows and cash crops. Beans and corn, corn and beans.

He quit crops when grain futures became a roller coaster he didn't want to ride. Forever climbing if you farmed a desk, forever falling if you farmed the dirt. He sold his plow and planter, leased his fields to one of the bigger operations. Bought a secondhand equipment trailer and backhoe, took side jobs. Dug stumps and ditches, laid culverts. Nothing big, but he did good work and word got around. Wheeled and dealed on an oil-burning dump truck and a well-worn bulldozer. Tuned them up, took the work as it came. It was a tough way to make a living. A slow way to make a living. But he'd always been good at tough and slow.

Maybe if the baby hadn't died.

The marriage sank into silence. They didn't fight. Wept less than you'd expect. These required energies largely unavailable. Grief deoxygenated everything. Once on a rainy morning in the muck of the barnyard, he had a vision of his soul as a thin sock in a leaky boot. He figured you couldn't pay a poet to put it any better.

At least they had their solitude. Hell was other people. Everybody with their advice and murmurs, their platitudes fit to be stitched on a pillow. He'd dip his head, press all the blood from his lips, somehow manage a thank-you while inside he raged. They wanted you to get past it so they could get back to comfortable. So they didn't have to avert their eyes. Or stand silent in the face of the unspeakable.

The barn, the baby.

Gone, never gone.

The farmer who leased Harold's cropland never showed up to farm it. In his stead came hired-hand agronomists with wands and laptops and satellite-guided monster machines, doing in a day what had taken Harold weeks. No wasted moves, everything programmed and precise. As opposed to all his years spent grubbing around. One fifteen-below morning back when he was still milking cows, the worm gear on the manure spreader fractured. He had to hustle off to the parts store because the cow poop was solidifying by the second, and if he didn't get it unloaded he'd have a half-ton shitsicle on wheels. His rust-bomb pickup truck wouldn't start until he crawled underneath and whacked the solenoid with a hammer. Halfway out the driveway, leaning in tight to the dash, eyeballing the road through a nickel-sized defroster porthole, he switched on the radio just in time to hear an evangelical finance guru declare, "Don't try to outwork stupid," and right out loud Harold said, "Well, that's really all I got goin' for me."

Side jobs. That's what it came down to. Digging koi ponds for orthopedic surgeons "into" country living, his wife stocking shelves at the Dollar Store, both of them hoping the lease money would cover the medical bills and the beef cattle would cover the taxes. Most every original local around here was stuck patching the gaps. Hell, at this point even meth head was a side job. He had grown weary of perfection and precision. He longed for worn leather, polished handles. What glacial marvels time and a callused palm could work against an axe haft.

Sometimes when another yoga-panted woman was griping down at him from her Denali over how much he undercharged for digging her prairie restoration patch, he faded into memories of Leon, the old three-fingered grader driver, and how all the kids in the schoolyard ran to the fence and waved as Leon passed, his stub-digit hands dancing across the levers, putting a crown on the gravel so the rain wouldn't puddle. The Grader Man, they called him, a capital-letter honorific and a fact. *A good blade man*, they'd say, back when even your lazy-ass tavern rat understood the weight those words carried. *The good old days*, he thought, and then—true to his recent resolution—immediately snuffed the reminiscence.

Thing is, he'd burned more time than he shoulda on that Starbucking Lululemon-clad woman's goddamn boutique prairie. He was, in fact, a good blade man. A damn good blade man. But these days that hauled no water. Might as well be the best butter churner, the best whittler, the finest Morse Coder in all the county.

He had his pride, so he did good work for those people. Not that they deserved it. Not that they could tell the difference.

He'd clung to the beefers. For the property tax discount, sure, but above all for his soul. You looked out over a pasture, you wanted to see cows. It was the one remaining thing that put peace in his farmer's heart: a grazing cow. The unhurried, natural stance of the animal, the soft rip of grass tugged from the earth. Later, the bunch of them on their bellies, tuck-legged and working cud. When he dared imagine an afterlife, cows and rumination were always a part of it.

But the cattle were gone now. Trailered off to the sale barn in early December. A dumb time to sell, but for three days straight he'd been abed with the flu, and her too. The flu, the hospital collection calls and bills piling, the backhoe hydraulics blown, the dump truck with a shattered differential, the ground froze snowless and solid, nobody wanting anything dug up anyway, soybean prices so far down the shitter the lease check was six months late and counting.

He didn't tell her. Just called the number on the card pinned to the wall beside the phone and waited for the rumble-rattle of the cattle jockey's aluminum gooseneck coming up the drive. He helped with the penning and loading, then turned his back and took off walking. Didn't stop 'til he hit the backmost property line. *Shit*, he said. *Fuck*. Then he leaned into the barbed wire and wept.

When the lease farmer finally showed, it wasn't with a check, it was to "renegotiate terms."

"We're in this together," said the lease farmer.

"The hell we are."

"Look, you don't really have a choice." The lease farmer's chest swelled a little as he spoke the words. His four-wheel drive pickup idled in the background. Harold had seen television ads for that vehicle and knew it to be equivalent in value to your entry-level Mercedes. Heated cup holders, and even more shamefully, it did the backing up for you. Raised and lowered its own tailgate. Which also had a cupholder.

"The *choice*," Harold answered, "is I'm gonna step inside the porch there then step out with a shotgun, at which point I will find you either waving a check or *gone*."

"Aw, that's no way to…"

It felt good to leave the lease farmer standing there, even better to step back out with the shotgun and see the dust from that fancy truck hanging in the air. All his life, nose to the grindstone, quietly playing by the rules, tortoise to the hare while the brash and brassy crowd bullied on through, it felt good to put one of them on the run. To take a shortcut. To *expedite* the situation.

But that lease money.

That was a stall from which he suspected he would not recover.

He could have sold the land. Sold it and come out even with the bank or just a shade ahead, just enough to buy a used camper out of somebody's yard. One of those roadside specials, parked parallel to the ditch and propping up a plywood sign spray-painted with a dollar-signed number and "O.B.O." Park at the end of the driveway, shade his eyes and peek in the windows, wait for the owner to show. Maybe play a little low-ball, suck his tooth, then pony up in cash. Hitch the trailer to his truck, pull it to one of those places along the interstate where chicken-legged patriots in Velcro shoes park in camp chairs and bitch about the state of the country that provided them a five-dollar camp chair and a place to plop it.

Sell the land, he thought, *and then what would I have? A whole new world, and no place in it for me. Nope, hangin' on to it. Every last acre. Not out of desperation but out of spite. Let it go to brush and weeds. Drive the digital agriculturalists and developers mad. Put some stop to progress. Delay it, anyway. The equivalent resistance to flicking a booger into a jet engine, but it's all the friction I can provide.*

Already the outer edges of the empty bean fields were sprouting popple whips. Meanwhile, after sundown the horizon to the west glowed with encroaching fitness centers, brewpubs, and mitotic apartment complexes.

Chapter Two

Another morning, another foot of snow.

Last time they watched TV together, the local news trio was oh-my-goshing the chances of an all-time 24-hour record accumulation. He was unnerved by the whiteness of their teeth. The weather woman's eyebrows seemed to have been inscribed on her skull with baler grease. It bemused him to think of these pandering electron mannequins as actual humans. Chit-chattering back and forth in the wake of the forecast, they goofed and feigned dismay, then knit their brows and adopted parental tones to dole out storm warnings as if death infected every snowflake.

He'd stood up and said *Jesus Christ* and kicked the screen in. She hadn't said anything, just sat there and was still sitting there when he drove his arms into his chore coat and strode outside.

You've become a true bastard, he thought to himself while staring at the empty feedlot. He knew they both had a hand in building the wall between them, but what in God's name kept him from even trying to reach over? How can you hold the balm in your hand and not unclench your fist?

Later, as they ate roast beef and potatoes at the kitchen table, the sound of her chewing made him unreasonably angry, but he was too stubborn to say so. They went to bed in silence, and he lay awake for hours, his anger having crimped itself into a knot of shame.

He pushed open the door. It swept a protractor arc through the snow. Shovel in hand, he stared at the white yard. He knew her body was there just off to his right, just in front of the porch swing where they'd held the baby and swung side-by-side in that briefest of springs. He stared straight ahead, his breath evaporating before his eyes. He set to clearing the steps.

Out of habit, he did the sidewalk, then he cleared a path to the chicken coop. He took his time with it. Got in rhythm: drive the blade into the snow, lift, and flick. *Drive, lift, flick.* In the deeper drifts, he shoveled the same place twice. Insert the blade midway to scoop the top, then skin it flat along the earth for the rest.

Every time he hoisted the shovel, he blew air, pursing his lips for resistance. It was a habit dating to his youth, formed after watching his father potter around the barn, bent double in the wake of hernia surgery. He was thinking in terms of a pressure relief valve, hypothesizing that the exhalation diverted pressure from any weakness in his abdominal wall. It was an idiosyncratic postulation, nurtured during long hours of toiling alone. Like most souls who operate in isolation, he had accumulated a plethora of pet theories never tested beyond his own mind. He took satisfaction in working these thoughts like a cow does a cud.

He used a standard snow shovel. Straight handle, steel blade. Once his wife had come home from town having bought one of the newer ones with the handle curved in the shape of a lazy "S." He disliked that shovel as a matter of both aesthetics and function. It looked loopy. Cartoony. Unserious. The design was intended to spare the lower back, and in fact one did have to bend less, but the balance was all off. The odd curve threw a sway into the handling. A quaver in the rhythm of the fling. Uncertainty in the basics.

He had surrendered certainty a long time ago but instilled order where possible. The square edges of his shoveling, for instance. He was precise, careful to shave the sides of the footpath, scrape the ground clean. Squaring things off was a means of honoring the task. It also gave him a measure of peace. The straight edges framed the snow, framed the work. Through his sweat, he recalled some philosopher once said, "we tend to think in terms of space; we are geometricians all."

He was a well-read child. His mother subscribed to a service providing library books by mail, and from a young age she let him choose from the catalog. He loved it when the books arrived in their padded sheaths, a recurring Christmas. Mostly he preferred cowboy stories and biographies of fighter pilots, but in his late teens he developed an accidental and amateur interest in philosophy after his English teacher assigned a reading from Montaigne's *Essais*. Harold inadvertently read the wrong pages, and instead of whatever he expected a French philosopher might write about, he found references to sex and farts. This was silly and appealed mostly to his dumb teen prurience, but it also implied that philosophy might be accessible and relevant even for a horny rube in barn boots.

And so he salted some philosophy titles in with the Red Baron and Eddie Rickenbacker exploits and Max Brand quick-draw hoo-hah. It gave him something to think about while waiting for the milker bucket to fill. Or the manure spreader to empty. Or—if he was feeling dramatic and had been reading Kierkegaard—to die.

Yah, he thought, the habitual self-deprecation kicking in, *and yet here you are, just a shithead shoveling snow.*

Upon reaching the coop, he cleared the door and drew it open. The hens blinked at him, then closed in to peck the snow from his boot toes, a sign they were thirsty. He pulled the lid from the plastic drum where the feed was stored and scooped out the day's ration, then headed back to the house for water.

While filling the bucket in the kitchen sink, he envisioned her leaning into this spot as she so often had, waist at the counter, hands in the suds, looking out the window to the valley below. Most winter mornings by the time he had the stove stoked, she had the chicken water bucket filled and waiting by the door. He had never requested she do this. Never *told* her to do this. She was simply exercising garden-variety thoughtfulness. Not in subservience but in graciousness. He cringed at the memory in light of all the times he just grabbed the bucket and trucked it outside. Not even a grunt of thanks. *How is it stubbornness suffocates shame,* he wondered. He would try now and then to reciprocate but always fell short. Sourness entered his belly. The slightest comment sent him off into the dark weeds for hours. There was no raging, no cursing or yelling, just a resentment that seeped like swamp gas and smothered everything. *Never laid a hand on her,* he thought, then immediately, *What the hell kinda standard is that?* Neither had he ever raised his voice against her, but then misery is rarely a matter of decibels.

It had become a function, not a marriage. When he woke to find her dead beside him, he had little reaction. He was terrified sometimes at his loss of emotion. If it came to be that St. Peter was waiting up there at the gate the way they used to preach it on Sundays, a berobed apostle standing behind a podium in the clouds running his index finger down the big reservation book, well, Harold figured his soul was toast. All the philosophy books in the world don't mean diddly if it turns out the preachers were right. Based on his willy-nilly reading and the dictionary, Harold supposed he was a humanist—a *diffident* humanist—but in fact it was his own homemade crown of multifaceted imperfections that drove him to doubt anybody had the straight goods. Contrasting the Bible he was raised on against the one waved like a pom-pom by politicians and holy hucksters had only reinforced his affinity for kindhearted doubters. True believers came at you with block-letter certitude, as if God communicated solely via stone tablet, but when pressed spent undue energy weaving and warping their favorite verses to retrofit the contradictions at hand. For all their raving against the dread liberal arts, Harold figured your average evangelist functioned at a *magna cum laude*-level of postmodern deconstructionism. Choose your commandment, choose your interpretation. When "thou shalt not kill" and the castle doctrine face off with nothing but a screen door between 'em, what is the nature of Truth? Armed with a Bible in one hand and a gun in the other, only a sucker turns the other cheek. *Ah well*, thought Harold, *there's more than one way to bend the macaroni.* As an aphorist, Harold maintained about a C average, lumbered as he was with a tendency towards dumb puns and echolalia.

The water was halfway up the bucket when out of the blue it occurred to him that she might have killed herself. She had never spoken of it, and there were no signs. But he was ignorant of plenty. He recalled she kept a bottle of prescription sleeping pills in the bed stand. A grief counselor had arranged for them during their only session. She had taken one and slept deeply but woke feeling disconnected and unrested, and as far as he knew, she had taken no more.

He shut off the faucet and made his way down the hall to their bedroom. The pill bottle was still in the drawer. He dumped the pills on the bureau top and pushed them one by one into a new pile, keeping count. Then he compared his count to the number on the label. Short by one. So she hadn't overdosed. He scooped the pills back into the bottle, capped it, and returned it to the bed stand. He had read something on the internet once about a medical study indicating you truly could die from a broken heart. In that case it wasn't suicide but rather slow murder.

Back at the sink he wondered how he should mourn her. Or if he could. All this self-examination and he kept coming up cold-blooded. In fairness, they had been bled of their capacity to grieve. Every edge had long been dulled. The pain—when it arose—was sharp as ever. But the ability to place it in any sort of relatable frame, or to even cradle and rock it, had long ago dwindled. *Entropy*, he thought. *Ennui.* Then he grunted in disgust. *Fancy four-dollar words, son, but what you got here is simply self-pity.* In short, he had failed to keep her safe. Failed to provide. The refrigerator had never gone bare, no check—even in the worst stretches—had gone overdrawn, but regarding the provisions of heart and spirit, he had quite simply walked off the job.

The tap water overflowing the chicken bucket drew him back to the present.

The hens gathered round as he filled the waterer, beaks tapping at the spring-loaded steel nipples, then raising their heads to bounce the water backward down their gullets. A heating element embedded in the base of the unit kept it from freezing, hardly rocket science but a luxury in that he didn't have to stomp ice out of a rubber pan every morning.

He gathered the eggs. Having forgotten to bring the basket he placed them in his coat pockets. This was a bad idea as with all his freelance philosophizing he was quite absentminded and had more than once forgotten the treasures in his pockets until he smashed them. He could have carried them in the empty water bucket, but he didn't want to moisten them. His mother taught him that the eggs were coated in a natural antibiotic barrier. A "bloom," she called it. In fact if you lifted a hen off an egg immediately after she laid it, you'd see the shell glistening wet. The slime air-dried to matte almost immediately and formed a microscopic membrane. City cousins were shocked to see eggs sitting out unwashed and unrefrigerated when in fact they were fine. Washing the eggs broke the barrier and might even introduce bacteria through the porous shell by capillary effect.

Thank you, Captain Tangent, he thought. *Although as opposed to your fat crayon philosophizing, your egg knowledge has some functional application.* He had long chewed over Aristotle's declaration that the unexamined life was not worth living. He had come to deeply agree, but that didn't mean he could recommend it. Even Kerouac said you don't have to torture your consciousness with endless thinking. In fact Harold's amateurish examination of humans and history fed his hopelessness. Of what worth was it to plumb the layers of existence when the world's privileged hordes were content to skate along on the surface of a touch screen? Or slide through life on the grease of their own smug exudations? Or the secondhand grease of star-spangled draft-dodgers peddling hot water heaters, bald eagle throw rugs, and resentment.

One night after making a late run to the veterinarian, he passed by the tavern and saw the regulars lined up shoulder to shoulder where the world was, if not their oyster, their pickled egg, and he wondered if it was terribly wrongheaded to leave nothing lasting on this earth but a nickel sized spot of polished wood where your elbow rested on the bar at happy hour for thirty straight years. *All my anemic overthinking, all my books and eyestrain,* he thought, *when perhaps inner peace was readily available in sixteen-ounce doses and a paper boatful of jalapeño poppers.*

"Self-pity is the last refuge of weenies," he declared aloud, but the chickens weren't listening. Spinning on his heel, he returned to the house, where he emptied his coat pockets of intact eggs (victory!), hung his sweat-damp stocking cap to dry on a nail beside the wood stove, and dipped out a bowl of stew. En route to eat on the couch he stopped at the bookshelf. Throughout that last half hour of moving snow he'd been trying to recall something he'd read some time ago. Something tied into the idea that the ability to perform straightforward tasks via simple solid skills honed through experience, observation, and physical exertion was no longer useful. Or worse, irrelevant. Certainly devalued. He placed the bowl on the floor and began to search the shelves, then the random stacks on the floor.

He was useless at retention and recitation. Rather, he had always visualized quotations in terms of location in the manuscript and placement on the page. He might not recall the chapter, but he could visualize the thickness of the leaves to the left and right sides of the split, the shape of the paragraph, and the location of a word relative to the line break. For all that, it took him thirty minutes of searching before he located the book. *Outworking stupid*, he thought. Then again, what else did he have to do?

The book was at the bottom of a pile. He recognized it by the design of the spine. *Story of Philosophy*, by Will Durant. In memory he envisioned the line as early in the manuscript, so he pinched the first few pages, opened them, and began to scan. Sure enough, in short order he spotted it on page 19: "…our means and instruments have multiplied beyond our interpretation."

He flipped back to the copyright page. 1926. Ha! What he'd give for the means and instruments of a century past. An image came to mind of the farmyard—his farmyard—on a summer afternoon the day this book was printed. Instead of the driveway, a dirt two-track, flanked and framed by elms. The twinned paths sunned and shaded in the very manner for which the much-maligned term "dappled" was intended. At pasture, a scatter of cows. A crisscross of slow-worn paths converging at the barnyard gate. A wooden wheelbarrow propped against a slatted corn crib. Sparrows, chirruping. And stowed in the horse barn, the first steel-wheeled tractor. Change, yes, but change in low gear. Everything still nuts and bolts. Everything learnable. Sortable. Repairable by one man. *Or woman*, he thought, out of late habit. He had always been quick to credit her for all she did to help them hold the farm.

They had never made out a last will and testament, but when they discovered the baby was coming, they printed a form from a website and began filling it out, intending to finalize it with an attorney in town. The instructions accompanying the form revealed a quirk in Wisconsin law—since Harold was still a bachelor when he inherited the farm from his father, it wasn't subject to the state's marital property laws, which otherwise make property owned by one married person the property of both. Legally speaking, she was not a joint owner. They agreed this was ridiculous—they had always thought of the farm as *theirs*, but the law said it was only *his*. Harold made a note on a Post-It and affixed it to the do-it-yourself form, intending to have the attorney sort it. Now she was gone and the baby was gone, and the half-finished document was lost in a stack of crap somewhere, and it didn't matter.

He imagined the farmer of 1926 tuning his tractor using a standard screwdriver and wrench set, then flashed forward to the khaki crew touch-screening their soybeans. That bunch wouldn't know a pitchfork if it jabbed them in their shrunken pleat-covered nuts. Harold's ability to lean into the flank of a Holstein, lay a hand on her udder, and detect a pending mastitis was irrelevant in the age of in-line testing. His facility with a scraper blade was no match for a "smart" grader tweaked by satellite. His knack for judging the moisture content of hay by twisting a handful and listening to the crackle was rendered moot by some tech school grad with a probe.

He turned his head to spit, then remembered he was in the house. The depth to which some evocative memories—even *imagined* memories of the farm as it was before he was born—overtook his senses and knocked the breath out of him. Left him adrift on a wave of yearning. But what good is it to pine for sweet yesterdays when there is suffering in the present? He remembered how his eyes widened the first time he read the Portuguese word *saudade*—a longing for things irretrievably past—and how as a youth that longing suffused him with keening and sweetness but nowadays led to wretched paralysis. The Welsh word *hiraeth* expressed a similar emotion, and the Germans spoke of *Weltschmerz*. Raised as he was by callused-handed stoics, these feelings embarrassed him. Fundamentally speaking, you can't clean the cow barn while breathlessly yearning.

In an effort to get back on track, he tried to imagine all the forgotten hardships of farming one hundred years ago. He knew better than to glorify hard labor. He'd slogged enough himself. Was *still* slogging. But this didn't alter his suspicion of anything he couldn't understand at a cellular level or couldn't fix with basic physics and blunt instruments. The speed and ease at which so many formerly arcane tasks could now be executed were unavailable to him because he had no facility with the intermediary technology: *our means and instruments have multiplied beyond our interpretation.* There was a pinching irony in the fact that any soft-palmed collegiate could sink a plow to the proper depth more efficiently than he. The new breed knew nothing of the plow but knew where to download—or was it upload?—the program. A single click and you've upgraded the grader. Harold knew how to get the most from wood and iron but was as useless as a city kid at a greased pig contest when it came to digital implements. He had clicked around on the Internet some and had a working understanding of email, but that was quill and ink at this point.

He remembered how the Peterson's Implement crew used to scoff at college-bred city folk. How everyone snickered behind the back of the first farmer to shell out for a computerized grain combine, especially when it turned out to be glitchy. Somehow all those old-timers had gone deaf to the echoes of their grandfathers' derision of tractors, all their hee-hawing about how no "contraption" would ever replace a solid draft horse. Of course the glitches were shortly resolved, combine computer screens became standard equipment, and good luck keeping up, old-timer.

The stew had gone cold. He dumped it back in the pan, gave it a stir, re-served himself, and took the book and bowl to the couch. Recalling another relevant passage, he set the stew aside and flipped forward several chapters then slowed to page-by-page until he spotted the paragraph matching the shape he sought:

> It is with instincts as with organs; they are the tools of the mind; and like all organs that are attached and permanent, they become burdens when the environment that needed them has disappeared. Instinct comes ready-made, and gives decisive—and usually successful—responses to stereotyped and ancestral situations; but it does not adapt the organism to change, it does not enable man to meet flexibly the fluid complexities of modern life.

Well, hell, he thought. *I wonder when's the last time I met flexibly the fluid complexities of modern life.*
Probably when I dropped my damn flip-phone in the stock tank.
His cheek twitched at the joke.
It was the closest he had come to a smile in three years.
He closed the book, ate the stew, and fell asleep.

Chapter Three

The snow kept coming, each fresh fall a stratified irony in that winters had been laggardly of late. Patchy and broken by warm spells. Spring-like melts during what should have been months of solid freeze. Even this winter, for all its accumulations to date, had dawdled out of the gate. He was aware of the global warming talk, the controversy pitting science against gored oxen. Or golden calves. Locally, there was a general derision of experts. He tended that way himself. His whole disdain for tap-and-swipe farming arose from a knee-jerk populist knucklehead stripe. After generations of getting mud on your boots for a living you didn't take naturally to some tenured professor lecturing you over weather. But certainly something was a-shift, if not amiss.

And yet there was refreshment in this winter's relentless precipitation. Refreshment and renewal. Every dark and jagged thing pristinely draped. Every shard and imperfection smoothed. Everything beautifully, beautifully blank. One morning after another six inches had fallen, he leaned the shovel against the coop and waded down grade, where he had a view to the Jones farm in the valley below. He had known old man Jones, the patriarch. Harold was just a boy then, helping his father milk a dozen cows. By comparison, old man Jones, with his thirty-five top-grade Holsteins, was considered a major operator.

Today the elder Jones was boxed and buried. Under the direction of his two sons, the original operation had expanded into a complex housing five hundred cows fed on borrowed millions. The debt was just the Jones boys doing what they could to hang on and match the market. The original barn—an exact replica of Harold's before it burned—still stood square, crowded into a corner by all the modernity. There was a time when the sight of a barn in that style—hip-roofed, green-shingled, hooded at one end of the peak where the horse-drawn hay hooks shuttled bales through the maw of the mow—would have eased his mind. Put him in a reverie. Now he just saw it as one more monument to everything lost. The barns that did survive were either stone-fired pizza joints, wedding chapels, or caved in.

Harold recalled hiking down to the Jones place as a child to borrow milk filters. He had been awe-struck at the cleanliness within the barn; the walks limed, the walls whitewashed, every cow's tail brushed to a wiry plume, the sweet smell of premium feed, all the lights burning, not a dead lamp in the bunch. The milk inspector's certificate framed above the gleaming bulk tank, the milking machines scrubbed spotless and drying on a rubberized rack neat as the kitchen dishes. Harold's father did the best he could, but things were always slap-dash and hay-wired. There wasn't always time. There wasn't always money. The feed Harold doled out for his father's cows was dusty and ran a shade more to cob than kernel.

Old man Jones's place had always looked like a photo spread for *Hoard's Dairyman*, and in their own way the Jones boys had carried on their father's tradition—top-of-the-line equipment, trim buildings, neat fields, clean yard, everything in its place no matter the financial vacuum beneath the surface. You could see the pride in their operation. But everything about it was exponential. Expanded by factors.

The original barn was the source artifact amongst a tessellation of ever more youthful structures.

But today Harold spotted something amiss amidst the geometry. Something out of alignment. The loafing shed—a large structure built to protect cows from the elements between milkings—had collapsed.

Harold knew what had happened. The snow. These giant, flat-roofed sheds, you got enough accumulation, down they went. Pancake city. All that surface area, all that water weight. From the road it looked like a Christmas card, but in fact it was an unbearable load. He could see three figures slowly circling. The two brothers, he figured, and an insurance adjuster. Old man Jones was the type that paid his bills on time and gave to the church and got most of his debt handled in that sweet spot through the 60s and 70s before Richard Nixon's Secretary of Agriculture told farmers to "get big or get out," and everything went to financing hell. The Jones boys took over in the late 90s and didn't just get big, they got huge. Erecting the loafing shed would have been a business decision as much as a family decision. If those boys were like their old man, it was likely that shed was fully insured, and a fresh one would rise within the month.

There was a time when something like this happened—a fire, a silo collapse, a death in the family—and everyone would show up to help. Bring their John Deeres and Internationals fitted with scrapers and loaders, maybe a backhoe and a straight truck with a dump bed, but mostly just backs and hands. There'd be a big lunch spread. Sauerkraut and bologna, fat loaves of unsliced bread, knobs of butter, homemade pickles. For dessert, vanilla ice cream topped with rhubarb and strawberry sauce. Nowadays you might get help, but lunch would be someone running for soda and subs from the gas station, and at the mid-afternoon Twinkies break, everyone would poke at their phones before announcing they couldn't stay because they had a thing, even though everyone knew they were going home to poke at their phones.

You still heard talk about country neighbors. And there were still folks who would show up and stay and return the following day. It happened. A farmer wound up in the hospital during harvest, the others showed up to get the corn in. But these attitudes had waned with technology and multiplicity. No need to talk to the neighbors now that everyone had everything they needed on-screen, plus free shipping. The last time he visited the local fire hall, the chief said the village was growing, but the new citizens drove in and out of their attached garages, and no one saw anything of them in between. The fire trucks and ambulances were down to skeleton crews, mostly seniors. You had octogenarians straining to lift cots full of fifty-year-olds with chest pain.

The wind picked up, and his eyes went watery, blurring the Jones tableau. He blinked hard, recalling how as a child on muggy summer days he'd stand on this spot and study how the natural haze turned the distant hills blue. He was deep in his cowboy book phase back then, and one of his favorites was *To the Far Blue Mountains*. Being a Wisconsin farm boy, he'd never really given the title consideration beyond the poetry of it. Then one day he was out here raking hay and gazing off across the land when the realization clicked into place. *"Ah!"* he had said, then laughed at himself for the obviousness of it. Then he laughed again for talking out loud in a hay field. Aboard a roaring tractor, no less.

Off to his left—east of the coop if you were talking points of the compass—the land was scored by a ravine. It cut sharply enough into the earth that you could back to the rim and tip trash over the edge, and for decades that's what the farmers and settlers had done. In the days when there were no landfills, back-forty dumps were a cherished tradition. In fact, with the recent proliferation of recycling charges and dumping ordinances, they were making a comeback. Harold had dutifully trucked his trash to the dump and had even acquiesced when his wife signed up for the county recycling program, but his father had used the ravine for decades, as had the farmer who owned the place prior. It wasn't just base trash; the ravine contained a fair amount of old implements and iron. Harold had pondered winching some of it out and hauling it to the local salvage yard, but scrap prices had been in the crapper for over a year now.

It had been a while since he'd nosed around down there. When he was a boy, it was one of his favorite places. He'd poke about for hours, unearthing treasure. Old coffee tins, glass motor oil jars, a vintage feed scale. A moss-covered work boot. A rusty fly spray fogger. A chipped hatchet head. He'd whittled a fresh handle for the hatchet, sharpened the blade on his father's bench grinder, and was still using it the last time he busted ice for the beef cows.

Harold swiveled his head and took in the land his father had willed him. From up here he could see nearly every square foot. A hundred-sixty acres run end-to-end by the ridge his buildings stood upon. The ravine was an anomaly; most of the topography fell away gently in humps and wrinkles. There was a little crick in the valley. A *creek* the newcomers called it, but *crick* felt easier on his tongue. It was the way he grew up talking. People heard you say *crick* they thought *hick,* but upon reflection and in summary he didn't give a shit.

How he loved running water as a child. Then he grew up and never took the time to sit with it. Never hiked down hand-in-hand with her to wade barefooted, embrace with the cold water chuckling around their ankles. All that land, and he and his wife had rarely walked it. He wondered sometimes if the much-vaunted midwestern work ethic was simply a means of emotional avoidance.

Immediately he snorted. *If?*

They had long planned a trip out West. She wanted to see the Badlands. He wanted—literally and without irony—to see some far blue mountains. See if they looked anything like the illustration on the cover of that cowboy book. He turned away from the horizon now and looked uphill over his shoulder, the farmhouse snow-snugged to the windowsills, the driveway drifted in tight. A brow of snow frowning over the eave of the three-season porch, where—he knew, though he couldn't see it from here—her body lay. He turned back to the valley. There were no blue tones today. The air was sun-blanched and clear. It seemed inconceivable it could ever hold a haze. The hills were bleached dunes stubbled with sticks.

Never made it out West.

Never made it out back. Or down to the crick.

My God, he thought, *life just up and evaporates.*

Then, after a moment, *And if somehow she lived again why would she ever forgive me.*

The three figures moved away from the imploded loafing shed and toward a vehicle parked on the drive. One figure separated, entered the vehicle, and drew the door shut. A moment later, Harold heard the thump of it. The other two men moved in tight and bent forward at the waist, hands stuffed in their coat pockets. That's how it went around here, the parting confab through the driver's side window. Even on a day as cold as this. Harold knew the ceremony well, having participated in it since childhood. After a time the men straightened and stepped back. The vehicle carved a Y-turn and departed. Somewhere a check was already as good as cut. Still, as he watched the Jones boys disappear into one of their several sheds, he felt no envy. Imagine dealing with all those cows and commas and so much of the enterprise locked in leveraged service to distant blue-toothed futures jockeys who wouldn't know cow shit if you packed it in their topsiders.

You are being petulant, he thought. *And grandiose.*

He figured he'd better check his own buildings. Specifically, his pole barns. He owned a pair of them. One red, one brown. Set as they were slightly downhill on the opposite side of the ridge, they weren't visible from the chicken coop. Harold returned up the path he had just cleared, leaned the shovel against the porch, then waded off the sidewalk toward a line of spruce trees running between the crest of the ridge and the pole barns.

It dated him, that term. These days pole barns were generally referred to as steel sheds or "post frame" buildings, but back when his father hired them built, the concept of a barn-sized structure composed by planting a series of tall poles capped with rafters and sheathed in corrugated steel was still relatively novel.

One of Harold's last backhoe jobs was for a wealthy architect who hired him to rearrange a set of decorative boulders amidst the shrubbery surrounding a cavernous riding stable. Afterward, when they were settling up, Harold said, "Nice pole barn." He truly intended the compliment. The architect stared at him blankly for a beat, then, as if dictating from behind a lectern, declared, "It is a custom barndominium-slash-hippodrome." Harold waited for the slow grin that would concede the absurdity of the extravagant jargon, but after an uncomfortable straight-faced silence, the man slipped an iPhone from his velveteen corduroys and said, "Do you accept Apple Pay?" Omnipresent, Harold thought, were the signs that contemporary culture was leaving him in the dust. "Nope," said Harold, and handed the man an invoice scribbled out on a carbon paper slip.

Harold kneed his way through the snow, following the unplowed drive path that passed through a gap in the spruce until he could see both pole barns.

The news was not good.

Each roof was mantled in snow deep enough to frost a tall man's apricots.

Shit, he thought. It was no joke, that much snow on a pole barn roof. The cumulative weight was remarkable. The Jones's weren't the first to suffer a collapse. He wondered how many cows they'd lost. He had a vision: half their herd crushed, the other half bawling like hell. Bad as his barn fire but in a deep freeze. He stared at the roof again. He had to clear that snow.

Last year a man died plummeting from the roof of a cattle shed while clearing it with a snowblower. That kind of story entertains centrally heated chuckleheads who chortle at the idea of some rube jack-strapping a Toro SnowMaster to the weather vane, but they are ignorant gigglers who've never known what it is to wait for a milk check when the kid is sick, the financier is a vulture, and your last corn kernel just hit the bottom of the feed bin like a death rattle. That snowblowing farmer was fighting a war of survival with the weapons available. Likely so far underwater financially his eyebrows drowned. You didn't take chances like that because you were a daredevil or a boob, you took chances like that because losing the barn meant losing the farm.

The stakes were nowhere near that high for Harold anymore. In fact, as he stood there with his head cranked back, trying to calculate the tonnage of the beveled white sheet cake, there was a part of him that cherished the fantasy of letting the whole works go down. *That'd take the pressure off*, he thought. Originally intended to house farm machinery and young stock, the pole barns had transmogrified over time into capacious catch-alls, each with its own gravitational pull. In short, they were packed with crap. The whole mess had been under-written for years by the phrase, *Some day I'll...* But those three dots might as well be the Grand Canyon. The dump truck was busted. The backhoe was busted. His wife lay dead on the porch, and he had done nothing. He couldn't imagine doing business with the public again. Couldn't imagine digging one more goddamn koi pond. *Let it all fall in a hole to hell*, he thought. But even as the words scrolled through his head, he knew he didn't have the guts. Residual practicality ruled.

Generations of grindstone genetics—manifest in concrete thinking, rebar stubbornness, and crowned with a barbed wire halo—compelled him by reflex to struggle against some possible future. He figured it was time to fire up the torpedo heaters.

Chapter Four

Returning to the house, Harold grabbed a set of aluminum snow-shoes and bushwhacked through the drifts down to the red pole barn, where the heaters were kept.

He opened the door and flipped the lights on. It was all darkness until his eyes adjusted, and immediately he wanted to close them again. It wasn't an overt hoarding situation, but the cumulative effect was so close as to fail the distinction. There were the essential tools and implements, a workbench and vise, coffee cans filled with nuts and bolts, boxes of nails, and of course the dump truck and back-hoe and other machines of his self-employment but also piles of junk and stacks of boxes. An assortment of 55-gallon drums, teetering columns of nested 5-gallon buckets. Racks of pipe and rolls of tub-ing. Odd lots of lumber. A mound of salvaged insulation reeking of mouse pee.

He'd picked up a lot of this stuff at auctions. He remembered when and where he bought every item, how he always figured he'd do this or that with each one. Now they were totems to all he had failed to accomplish. Git 'er done, his people were wont to say, and when you added it all up, he hadn't. At least not in proportion to the time spent doing the dead man's float in a pool of ennui. Just off to his left un-der plastic were a set of high-back kitchen chairs and a Murphy bed. Nabbed those at the Kollwitz sale. Leaned against the table saw, six solid wood antique doors fitted with enameled knobs. Rescued those from a house he'd helped burn for training purposes back when he was on the fire department. Back when he felt part of a larger community. The plan had always been to incorporate the chairs and Murphy bed and doors into their dream house. Their dream house being a modern version of the simple L-shaped farmhouse. Fashioned after the past only with good plumbing and maybe a walk-in shower. Then the baby died, and the dream house with it. Everything but misery seemed a frivolity. Somewhere under their bed was a notebook with lists and sketches and floor plans. After the funeral, they never looked at it again. Just burrowed more deeply into the old house. It became a bunker. *Hunker*, he thought, an involuntary rhyme. The house became a hovel, comfortable only in the sense that it kept the outside world at bay. It began to slouch and slant. He couldn't bring himself to do the simplest repairs. A length of soffit detached two years ago and still clacked against the bedroom window when the wind rose. Rain seeping through a hole in the basement wall had socked three inches of silt around the base of the hot water heater, and now it was rusting. The kitchen window was askew, the frame having succumbed to dry rot, leaving one corner of the window itself to settle aslant. On summer evenings, moths slipped through the gap. In winter, snow. The house became a monument to neglect.

He shook his head. *What's your point*, he thought.

A torpedo heater resembles a stubby howitzer piggybacking a fuel tank. Harold owned a pair: one on wheels and one with a carrying handle. He located the first behind a collapsed stack of mildewed books, the other beneath a torn tarpaulin.

Making space at the center of the pole barn, he arranged the heaters butt to butt, one aimed toward each sidewall. He cleared a path before their respective muzzles, setting aside anything that might catch a spark. About five feet out, he propped a plywood panel against a sawhorse. This reminded him of the bicycle jumps he used to rig as a kid. How the first time he built one he expected to fly but in fact did a violent faceplant and broke his forearm. This had cured him of flashy moves for a lifetime. The plywood deflected the heat toward the eaves, where it would then roll toward the peak, heating the steel roof as it rose. Heat rises regardless, but over the course of many winters Harold had learned this little trick expedited the process. You spent less time heating the floor.

After running a split-tail extension cord to the heaters, Harold filled each with kerosene. He had never cared for the smell of either kerosene or diesel. Straight gasoline, hell, he huffed it as a kid on a regular basis while refilling the old man's John Deere. Not for a buzz; he was too dumb, sheltered, and square to know of true hardcore huffing, he just liked the way it smelled. Later in life he read a quote in which the country singer Waylon Jennings said the very same thing about cocaine, and he supposed in this methamphetamine age no one would believe he hadn't huffed to get high, but in all his calf-brained ignorance, he really did simply enjoy the aroma. Diesel and kerosene held a caustic edge; they were noxious on the nose. Gasoline hit like a vaporous cushion. So he'd sniff a fully-leaded snootful as he waited for the tank to top, then cap it and carry on. But put gasoline in your torpedo heater and you go for a rocket ride, so in went the stinky kerosene.

Once both tanks were topped, he knelt and switched the first heater on. In the snow-insulated silence there was an electrical click, the fine hum of the pump, a *WHUFF!* of ignition, then the hollow jet-engine roar of the fan. He lit the second, then moved around front to watch the baffle slowly glow up a molten orange. A cloud of hot air swept past him.

Harold had come to rely on the torpedo heaters after failing at more standard measures during previous winters. He had tried to shovel the roof clear, but once he got up there he realized the square footage was far greater than he suspected, and the snow was too deep to push. Throw in the fact that it was a twenty-foot fall to the frozen earth if you went over the edge, and he just didn't have the appetite for it. He'd seen nifty videos on the internet of people undercutting the snow by sawing a rope back and forth, but they had tiny houses with steep roofs, not vast pole barns built to minimum pitch. In addition to the farmer who died running his rooftop snowblower, he had heard of another man hospitalized after stepping through a fiberglass skylight. Ruptured his scrotum on a cross truss and landed on his head. It was easier and safer to fire up the heaters.

The goal was to heat the tin roof just enough that the snow slid off. It didn't always work. If the temperature dropped too low the heaters couldn't get ahead. If the snow partially melted then refroze, it formed a sheet of ice that locked around the rubberized nailheads and wouldn't let slip. Harold checked the old Peterson's Implement mercury thermometer nailed to the post just inside the door: 28 degrees. Should be good.

Already the pole barn was warming. It was a fundamentally glorious thing, a torpedo heater. Loud and basic and atmospherically transformative. It even *sounded* hot. A blow dryer scaled up to set the curls on a wooly mammoth. He could never really explain why items of this nature gave him such pleasure. His raising, he supposed. It was why he loved old pickup trucks. A good knife. A bolt-action rifle. Layered into the pleasure of their simplicity was the way in which they counterbalanced his philosophical predilections. His susceptibility to fuzzy-headed mawkishness. The fact that he took joy from pushing dirt with a bulldozer ensured he'd never get completely lost in the clouds.

There was a decal pasted on the side of the heater. It featured a single declaration bracketed in red exclamation marks: !*NEVER LEAVE YOUR TORPEDO HEATER UNATTENDED*!

"Huh," said Harold and headed for the house.

By noon the pole barn eaves were dripping. By midafternoon a fissure appeared at the peak. Harold snowshoed back down to refill the kerosene tanks. When he stepped back outside and slammed the pole barn door behind him, the whole works let loose. The sheet cake split and calved with a screeching rush, the chunks breaking at the edge of the roof and tumbling in a series of rapid earthen thuds.

And then, silence. It occurred to him there was a joke percolating in the one-letter distinction between "calving" and "caving." Something about it being an "L" of a difference. Having been so morose for so long, the silliness of the thought caught him off guard. Furthermore, the clean sweep of the roof left him with a lightness of spirit he'd not felt in months.

In this spirit he set about transferring the heaters to the brown pole barn. In short order all his lightness went to sludge and scorch.

The row of spruce formed a natural snow fence. The flakes came kiting in on the prevailing wind only to hit the treetops and decelerate, and, like a drunk stumbling over a hedge, drop from the sky to accumulate in a leeside heap, burying the pole barns and the area between them. Most winters he would have kept the paths interconnecting the pole barns and yard plowed clear, but this grim season he had neglected the job. The swale was in-drifted and packed to the point he doubted he could bust through with his truck-mounted plow, let alone a snow shovel.

With no path cleared between pole barns, he lurched and lunged through the snow, dragging first one and then the other heater behind him. The experience was akin to running in a nightmare while tangled in bedsheets. Sometimes one snowshoe caught on the other, and he tipped into the drifts. In fighting his way upright, he left the impression of brawling snow angels. At one point he fetched an old ice fishing sled and strapped a heater to it, but the load was top-heavy, and every ten feet or so the whole works tipped sideways, draining kerosene into the snow. So he was back to lurching and dragging. It was an extended petulant tussle. He spit curses. At one point he considered rousing the bulldozer, but he'd have to run extension cords to the block heater, and even then he wasn't sure it would start. He berated himself for failing to keep up with the plowing.

Finally he had the heaters in place and lit. Exhausted, he made his way back to the house and fell asleep on the couch. At 2 a.m. he woke and snowshoed down to check the state of things. All was silent and still. The torpedo heaters had burned through their fuel and shut down. But when he played his flashlight beam across the roof of the brown pole barn it was slick and clean. Both of 'em good, then. He blew out his cheeks in relief and went to bed.

Chapter Five

He slept past dawn. By the time he rose, a fresh two inches had fallen, and more by the minute. When he stepped off the porch with the chicken water, the air was still, leaving the flakes to descend on their own lazy terms, as if lightning had struck a migration of moths. Now and then one touched down on his cheeks or nose. There was a sensation of melt and tickle.

At the coop he set the bucket down and trudged toward the tree line. The spruce and pine boughs were draped and sagging. The stripling sumac and lowermost apple tree branches were nubbed and nibbled, a sign that the deer could no longer paw through to grass. He stood stock-still in the absorbing silence. He had long suffered from hyperacusis of the soul. Noise and intrusion made him unreasonably angry. Here everything was dampened. Muffled. Soft. It was a comfort.

Then he thought of her. How the silence between them had been anything but a comfort. He looked back up toward the house. Every time he passed in or out the door, he was forced to pass her body. *As you deserve*, he thought. Like a drunk driver sentenced to visit the victim's grave as terms of parole.

He still had no idea what had caused her death. An aneurysm? Some internal bleed? Perhaps it was a simple heart attack: in his EMT class down at the fire department the instructor said women didn't always "manifest" the symptoms men do, although there was reason to wonder if women's symptoms had been adequately studied or prioritized.

Of course the cause of death was irrelevant. It was odd to be legally blameless for her death and yet understand he was wholly culpable. No, that wasn't quite right: his culpability was not for her death but rather the relentlessly dour atmosphere of her existence in the years prior. This was a crime far darker. He was guilty of denying tenderness. Turning away from tenderness. Cruelty does not require a raised hand.

A movement caught his eye. A fisher, humping through the snow. Weasels on steroids, his dad called them. Predator of rabbits, squirrels, and porcupines, and—given the opportunity—hell on chickens. For a single shaved second, it stopped and stared at him, its eyes black, its coat deep brown and glossy. Then it whirled and disappeared. In the stillness he heard individual snowflakes landing, the sound somewhere between *tick* and *shh*.

Back in the house he cracked the day's eggs into a pan. As they spattered, he studied the room. Neither of them had been particularly assiduous housekeepers, but now that she was gone, there wasn't even the pretense of order. Stacks of encrusted pans and dishes. The kitchen table buried in sales flyers, unopened junk mail, gloves, a scatter of tools, and a hydraulic jack he'd brought inside to warm so he could drain it and replace a leaking seal. That was a month ago. Now it was a paperweight atop a pile of unpaid bills gone translucent from the leaking fluid. Beneath where the phone used to hang was a cluttered desk and overflowing box of unsorted receipts. Might as well incinerate them. He couldn't foresee doing his taxes at this point.

In keeping with the theme of neglect, the house was capitulating as a whole. It creaked in ways it hadn't previously. A stair tread had come loose; the iron-stained tub shower still worked but only at one temperature and with the control at one position—half an inch to the left or right and it cut out. It had been that way for months because neither of them would call the plumber, neither of them wanting anyone to puncture the bubble of their mournful isolation, which they wore as widow's weeds.

On particularly cold mornings, frost formed along the baseboard; a crack in the plaster over the bed had widened; often when he stood still for a moment after banking the fire at bedtime, he heard mice askitter in the walls. Occasionally he'd spy one out in the open. One morning after sensing a movement atop his blankets, he raised his head to find a little gray fellow perched on his shins, looking right at him, unblinking. He'd discover nests beneath the stove composed of newsprint and vermiculite. Scat appeared like chocolate sprinkles in the silverware drawer. Now and then one of the rodents died behind the plaster. The smell peaked in three days then dissipated.

What a mess, he thought. Even when she was still alive, there were times he stared into the fire last thing at night and considered opening the stove door, shoveling coals across the carpet and walking into the woods as it all burned. But a fire would draw attention, and they wanted only to be left alone. Which they had achieved. Even in the presence of other people.

Even in the same bed.

He opened a can of beans and spooned them onto his eggs. Out the kitchen window the snow was falling ever more thickly. He'd have to get a jump on melting the pole barn roofs. If it kept up like this, he'd burn through his kerosene. The heaters would run on diesel in a pinch, and he had plenty on hand, but his heaters were older models; diesel would burn dirty and foul the works. These days the farm store on the outskirts of town catered mostly to hobbyists, but they still sold kerosene from a pump off to one side of the filling station. He dreaded the drive. Leaving the property at this point felt like breaking a promise.

The last time he went to town it was to renew the license for his dump truck. There had been a mix-up, and he was required to present himself at the DMV in person. He detested bureaucracy, but then he secretly reckoned the general deterioration of civil society was in no small part due to decades devoted to the denigration of civil servants. As if the person standing on an anti-fatigue mat behind the counter dealing with nonstop public truculence was jetting off to Turks and Caicos every weekend. As if every "nameless bureaucrat" didn't have a name. He once attended a state agriculture convention and found himself cornered beside a pesticide display by a man with a skinny belly and a fat belt buckle who speed-shifted from shooting the breeze about corn hybrids and rainfall into a rant about the nation rotting from within thanks to "freeloading welfare queens" mooching off "the system," and this not five minutes after the governor was roundly cheered for announcing a multi-million dollar expansion of soybean subsidies.

Harold himself harbored his own contradictions, constantly hung as he was between a fierce desire for unfettered independence and repulsion at what floated to the top of the pool in a so-called free market meritocracy. He wished he could believe everything he used to believe. Manifest destiny, for starters. Sainted Founders. American exceptionalism. He wished he could clap his hand over his heart, say the pledge, and feel his heart welling up with certitude and beer commercials. In some respects, he remained susceptible. He was, if not a rugged, a stubborn individual. But a preponderance of late evidence indicated that the country was being pawned by grifters and bellicose underachievers, and he was firm in his conviction that belt buckle dude was a bumptious double-talker.

Just inside the DMV door, a woman behind a desk took his name and gave him a number, like it was the meat counter at the IGA. He accepted the ticket grudgingly. *I bet*, he thought. Then she called his number inside of ten minutes, and he was out the door with his paperwork in twenty. That didn't make for much of a diatribe to share with the fellas down at the parts store.

He planned to head right back home, but when he exited the DMV, he caught a whiff of roasting coffee beans emanating from the brick storefront next door. He didn't drink coffee as a rule, but now and then he favored a cup, and thanks to the unexpectedly smooth experience at the DMV, he had the time. Furthermore, he was hungry, and hung in the window was the word SANDWICHES in neon.

The second he entered he knew he was a toad in a jewelry store. But he had stepped too far, which is to say he was stranded in that no-man's land between the entry and the counter. The woman behind the bar was looking at him expectantly, and there was no retreating without an obvious backtrack. Harold had an inborn horror of attracting undue attention in seemingly minor instances such as this. He teetered for a moment, but the woman smiled and said, "Hello!" One side of her head was shaved. Her remaining hair was dyed in chartreuse stripes, and a tattoo spilled down one bare shoulder. He shambled forward.

"What can I gitchya?" And a nose ring. She had a nose ring.

"I'm, um…"

"Take your time!"

He tipped his head back and scanned the chalkboard menu. The last time he felt this dumb he was boarding a jetliner with his wife for their one true vacation, an agricultural package tour to Hawaii. He had never flown and was having trouble finding his seat. The process—row number, seat letter—couldn't have been simpler, but he nonetheless found himself with his head at the same angle as it was now, blocking the flow of passengers as his scalp prickled and his ears burned. By the time he stowed his bag, he was sweating like he'd been stacking hay. As he fumbled with his seatbelt, his wife smiled at him. He just shook his head and scowled. He added this memory to the list of reasons she should have shot him in his sleep.

He snuck a glance backward. There were three coffee customers standing behind him. None were looking at the chalkboard. With a cold flush he realized they were regulars and already knew what they wanted. The back of his neck went damp. He lurched forward two more steps and braced against the counter with both hands.

"Jist a regular coffee," he said. "And…" He glanced at the chalkboard again. "And…a Chix Luv It." He had no idea what a Chix Luv It was, and he blushed when he heard himself saying it, but he was desperate to wrap things up.

"Potato or corn?"

"Ahh…"

"Chips. You get your choice of chips."

"Um. Potato." The sweat bumped yet again. Why did speaking such a simple desire before strangers feel like dropping his pants?

"Side of fresh fruit?"

"Yes." He had no desire for fruit. Didn't even know it was an option. He just wanted the questions to stop.

"Alright, sir, here you go." She spun a digital tablet toward him. It displayed the total. The coffee alone was crowding the price of an entire McDonald's Combo Meal. He offered a twenty-dollar bill. She took it and punched the cash drawer. He looked at the screen again. It displayed two rows of suggested tip amounts. She was already making change, so he stabbed at one, then flushed deeper red when he realized it was the lowest.

The woman re-did his change, handed it to him, then drew his coffee. He noted another smaller chalkboard propped against the muffin display. The words "Your Barista" ran along the upper border of the board, and below them in white chalk was written, "JerLuna, she/her." While he supposed his general frame of mind, favored reading material, and overall solitude kept his cultural references lodged more deeply in the early 20th century than was age-appropriate for even your standard old white guy, he had spent enough time online over the past decade to understand what the pronouns were about. He didn't react strongly either way and in fact wondered if they were flipped to "her/she" whether the subliminal effect might trigger an uptick in sales of chocolate muffins. He took pleasure in these tangential inanities and knew enough to keep them to himself. *Dad joke*, he thought, and his eyes flashed with tears. He blinked hard and fast to clear them. He so rarely thought of himself as a father. The baby was there and then gone.

JerLuna placed his coffee on the bar, her hand lingering on the handle when she noticed the moisture on his lashes. He ducked his head and grabbed for the mug, slopping the coffee. JerLuna ran a rag over the spill.

"Thanks," he said, turning away with the mug awkwardly propped between the fingertips of both hands.

"I'll bring your food out to you," said JerLuna at his back, as genuinely friendly as if he'd tipped her another twenty bucks.

He scuttled to the nearest table. His ears felt like they could roast corn. He'd been this way as a child. Panicky over the most mundane public attention. Grocery store checkout lines. The post office. Checking in with reception at the damn dentist. All he could think of was how he wanted to leave. He looked at his boots. Thank God he'd sold the beefers so he wasn't tracking cow shit. But the chickens! He rotated both soles inward for a quick inspection. Nothing.

He pulled out his phone just so he could keep his head down and stare at something but then felt provisionally more stupid because it was a flip phone. He squinted and stabbed around on it anyway. Pretended he was checking for messages. He couldn't remember when he'd last had a text. This drove him to actually check.

His wife. Over two months ago. "Supper," it said. Holy hell.

He snapped the phone closed and snuck a look around. The place was pretty much full, customers ranged around the tables and vintage furniture. Some were reading books. Some were sketching or writing in journals. Most were staring at their phones or laptops. A few feet from his table, a young couple sat side-by-side on a couch. Two girls.

Women, he corrected himself. They were sharing a pair of earbuds and giggling at something on a laptop.

The coffee shop building looked to have been an old factory or livery. The walls were exposed brick and hung with what he'd call oddball art: a stiff Civil War era family portrait in which every face had been replaced with that of a Star Wars character, a comic carved into a square of linoleum, a framed and hand-tinted photocopy of David Bowie's mugshot from an arrest in the 1970s, an illuminated tin sign declaring "NO DE-CAF!" And above the bar, a rainbow flag.

As a straight farm boy, he had come to understand the significance of the flag long before it was ubiquitous, thanks, ironically enough, to the radio in his pickup truck, where he first heard it held forth as an object of derision by an ascendant talk radio host. There was a time when he laughed aloud and pumped his fist in assent at what he heard from the radio man. So many pretentious balloons being pricked. So many sacred cows tipped. So much "common sense." But over time "common sense" morphed into poisonous smuggery. What he heard on the radio was cruelty, and lately around these parts, to call it cruelty, to do anything other than chortle in chorus, was to be seen as weak and likely seditious. What he once cheered as pithy repartee championing the working man slowly morphed into mockery and virulence interspersed with pitches for pillows, tankless water heaters, and vitamin supplements.

He'd sit in the yard with the engine off but the key switched on and try to imagine his father or old man Jones swallowing—let alone regurgitating—such obviously fraudulent blather. Perhaps they would have, they just didn't need to, living as they did in a world—a narrative, the intellectuals would call it—of their own shaping. He had come to understand the power of this critical distinction. Change precipitated fear, fear precipitated evil. He himself had miles to go and admitted part of his retreat from the world was driven by a fear of sticking his foot in his mouth over some cultural technicality. In the coffee shop, for instance, there was a poster pinned to the bulletin board beside his table announcing an event for "womyn," and although he felt like he'd made decent progress for a sheltered knucklehead, he hadn't made it to "y." He read somewhere once that "false etymology is no way to run a revolution" but had also reworked his thinking enough to suppose this begged the question of how many women—or womyn—were at the table when etymology was codified. Language evolves, today's Exhibit A being his usage of the phrase "begged the question," for which certain grammarians would still give you a good scolding despite knowing full well what you intended. Still, regarding his nervousness about the new rules, even at his unreconstructed level it seemed logical to proceed on the premise that sticking your own foot in your own mouth was light duty compared to a stranger's fist in your face. Or knee on your neck.

The young couple on the couch giggled again. He noted they were holding hands.

He took a careful, breathy sip of the coffee. It was remarkably good.

He had never told his wife when she had her dream house coffee table picture books and *Home Digest* clippings and construction plans open on the kitchen table, all her little notes scribbled out in pink ink, but he had always detested the term "dream house." As if you could sit there with your eyes closed and will the rafters into place. As if people of their ilk sat around hoping for such a thing instead of putting shoulder to wheel and earning it. *More like worked-our-asses-off house*, he'd think. Even if things had panned out, if they had the whole damn deal and petunias too, he figured he would have been a little unsure how to act in a house with a thermostat, clean windows, and a drywall echo.

JerLuna was at his elbow. "Here y'go," she said, setting his plate before him. "Can I get you anything else?"

"Nope. Thank you."

He ate the chips, then the fruit, and then turned his attention to the sandwich. There were cranberries in the chicken salad. Cranberries and almond slivers. He had not reckoned on this. It wasn't bad, just unexpected. The chicken and almonds went good with the coffee.

The young couple had noticed him. As he raised his gaze, they averted theirs. It was clear they were new at this, and his presence was chilling. His farmer boots, his ratty fire department cap, his obvious cultural clunkiness in this context, his squint when he read the "womyn" poster. It shamed him that they looked at him and weren't sure. He had been raised to believe a man and a woman was the only way to go if you wanted to go to heaven, but having reflected on the whole deal over time, he had come to believe humanity had found enough ways to cause itself pain, so let love abound.

He looked at the flag again. Cultural context aside, it was *pretty*. Easy—joyful, even—on the eyes. He despised bumper stickers and bumper sticker thinking (he once announced to the chickens that talk radio was just bumper stickers out loud; the birds blinked at him, awaiting their feed). For all his reading, he'd never been a writer, let alone a coffee shop poet, but he figured if he took it up, he'd attach a little rainbow sticker to his laptop lid just to put the young couples and others like them at ease. A coded courtesy.

They were studying him again, and he tried a small smile of reassurance but chickened out immediately and drove his eyes back down to his plate. *Goddammit, made it worse*, he thought. He grabbed his coffee and sipped the last of it. He badly wanted to scoff at what it cost, but in fact it was delicious and made his eyelids twitch.

He plucked up his courage and snuck to the bar for a refill. "Seventy-five cents," said JerLuna, and he gave her exact change. Her cellphone was on the bar faceup, and while she was drawing his coffee, a text pinged in and the screen lit up. "Call me," the text said. Behind the text bubble the screensaver was a photograph of JerLuna and another woman with a curly-headed toddler between them. All three were leaning into each other and beaming.

He snapped his gaze away just as she turned around. "Thanks," he said, taking the coffee and managing not to spill this time. She picked up the phone and stepped into the tiny kitchen. He wished he had nabbed a muffin. He settled for picking at a few stray slivers of Chix Luv It almonds. The second cup of coffee was good but didn't hit him like the first. He drank it too quickly and numbed his tongue. The young couple on the sofa were back to giggling. He gathered his dishes and mug and placed them in the bussing tub, which was in a small space between the bar and kitchen. He could hear JerLuna on the phone. She was crying. "But why now? After everything we…Yes, but you said…"

She peeked out to see if she had any customers waiting and caught him standing there with his mug and plate. He wanted to say something, but he couldn't. He put the dishes in the tub, placed a twenty on the counter, and fled.

Now here he was all this time later, standing solo in his squalor, the eggs burnt in the pan, wondering what news that phone call delivered. She had clearly been blindsided. How bizarre it seemed that he had peeked so deeply into her life thanks to coffee beans on the breeze.

The thirty minutes he spent in that shop were a cultural non sequitur. He was reminded of the Hawaii trip and how he marveled at the feel of sun on his chest in January, partly because it was January and partly because folk of his lineage and vocation rarely bared their chests to the sun. The bridge of your nose, the nape of your neck, the back of your hands, and that was it. On the beach you could tell the midwestern farmers by their gloves of tan and their fish belly foreheads. Sitting oceanside one afternoon, he experienced a moment of fascinating dislocation in which he wondered what his life would have been like if he had been born on the island. Instead, the sight of a pelican left him speechless, as if he had been dropped into a Time Life nature book. He enjoyed himself but quietly so, embarrassed as he was by the hee-hawing gawkery of his traveling companions, happy to bury their faces in tropical drink bouquets while comparing the height of sugarcane to field corn and allowing how this or that would never "go" back home. He wasn't morose, but he was wooden. This was before the baby, so it wasn't the worst of it, but it wasn't the best of it, either. Why was he always so goddamn *astringent?* He couldn't shake the nagging sense that if he'd just loosen his mood and kick up his heels and drink a ridiculous drink it would make her terribly happy, and yet still he held himself tight as a beetle, resolutely containing his outer self even as his inner self marveled over sea urchins and starfish and the sound of palm fronds clacking in a breeze.

What if writing bad poetry in a coffee shop notebook might be a source of joy akin to Hawaii in January? Why did he assume these things were not for him? Or that he'd be violating some stupid self-imposed clodhopper code? As he pinched up the last almond sliver of his Chix Luv It that day, he spied a young man with an oiled beard and waxed mustache composing verse with a fountain pen. Harold snorted softly. And yet as he stood here now in his own trash, he wondered: for all the lip service paid in his roughneck circles to the By God All-American work ethic and bootstrapping and doing it yourself, the beardo hipsters with their hand-tooled leather, repurposed barn wood, and homespun knitting were actually making real things from real things using old tools. Meanwhile the four-wheel-drive flag-wavers were wearing boots made in China and would prefer not to milk the cows. Raised to believe that hard work and cold winters built character, Harold had only now come to believe that in fact the world was overpopulated with assholes unlikely to improve their character no matter how deep the mercury dropped or how high the snow piled. Hell, as hard as he'd worked and as cold as he'd been as often as he'd been, how to explain away the anemia of his own character?

When he was a child, his mother lined the window sash with translucent blue glass insulators she'd collected along rural railroad tracks. Even now, when he envisioned them in a row with the outside light filtering through, he felt a visceral calm. This seemed a form of poetry. *What life might I have had*, he wondered, *had I not been a stubborn farm boy.*

Despite his relentless darkness, he had always maintained a grim gratitude. It was as if he understood his unhappiness. Accepted his unhappiness. There was amelioration in a few basic understandings: he was not imprisoned. He was not in physical torment. He was not being force-marched at the toe of a boot or the barrel of a gun. He was free to come and go. Hell, he was free to toddle right into town, grab a cappuccino, and sign up for goat yoga.

He could muster up excuses—the baby dying, the slow hemorrhage of the farm, the unrelenting inbound world—but *excuse* and *excusable* weren't the same thing, and he knew it. He had fostered his darkness at the expense of her light. Even as he settled for what he'd become, she worked for change. To grow. He'd see books on the nightstand. *Know Yourself and Grow. Dream and Live. Simplify Your Way to Happiness.* And after the baby, *Navigating Grief.* A new one every damn week. He'd get angry that she was looking for something he couldn't give. The anger acidified into a petulant inner monologue along the lines of *Go for it, good luck, if you can't find it on your own, you won't find it in those books.* He randomly opened one—*Dream to Declutter*—to a passage quoting a "feng shui psychic" describing how she could hear a messy house weeping. It was all he could do to keep from drop-kicking the book through their filmy bedroom window. He felt betrayed by her entertaining anything he termed as "woo-woo." He thought he had married a rock solid farm girl. They were long past talking about it. He could hardly advocate for his precious philosophers, being as he was Exhibit A to the self-indulgent futility of that path, and besides, who gets to define "woo-woo"? Might as well throw in with the lady who detected tears in the sock pile.

Once again he studied the dark mess of the house. He had worn a web of visible trails from the bedroom to the bathroom, to the kitchen, to the wood stove, to the couch, to the front door. What if perseverance was just us running ruts cut before we were born?

Cripes, he thought. *We circle our cages in ignorance.*

For the past couple of years, it seemed every thought he held veered almost comically toward the elegiac—a word he was not confident in spelling but knew was tied to expressions of sorrow or lamentation. He had first experienced this feeling after a run of funerals unlike anything he had previously encountered. A raft of old-timers he had come to think of as comprising the local pantheon had died, one after the other, in the space of a few months. Junebug Fossy, who ran the last general store in town before it got bled out by a big-box; Boobsie Jinks, the tractor mechanic who tossed him a crinkle-wrapped butterscotch whenever he tagged along with his dad to Peterson's Implement; Dick and Dixie, who ran the Dick'n'Dix Tavern for five decades, gone within three months of each other; Goldie Fitzwater, known to every local as "Angry Alice," who spent sixty years waiting tables at Hoot's Cafe. There was nothing dire or suspicious afoot with all these deaths, simply an actuarial confluence. But sitting through yet another service, he felt the mortal tide swamping his boat.

Prone as he was to noodle-headedness, he really didn't require a run of funerals to catalyze the ponderment of his own mortality, but so it went. The main effect was a reconsideration of his character and priorities. Or *life goals*, as he had read on the back of one of her bedside books. Or was it his *passions*? "Locavorism is my *passion*," declared a life coach for whom he had just filled a series of snap-together pre-fab raised beds from the big box store, and he curled his toes so hard he feared he'd claw through his boot soles. She stood oblivious to the residual mochaccino sprinkles dotting her upper lip.

Throughout the funeral cluster he was never at the center of grief; in most cases he simply shuffled through the visitation line, dropped a card, paid his respects, and drove home. What unsettled him was the loss of his own tangible history. He didn't just lose Junebug, he lost the sound of Junebug slamming the dice cup down on the cafe counter and Angry Alice cussing Junebug out. He lost any chance at reviving the past.

Back before the baby was born and they could find humor in such things, his wife once prevailed upon him to watch a DVD of *Four Weddings and A Funeral*. He was giggling along and thus blindsided by the death scene. When the young man at the church lectern recited W.H. Auden's "Funeral Blues," tears slid from his eyes.

Later he dug around in his book collection and read up on the poem, learning among other things that it was the very definition of elegiac. He was more surprised to discover it was originally written as satire, conceived upon the premise of mourning a dead politician; the first two stanzas are all that remain of that version. In light of the drooling inanities issuing from the current ruling class, his visceral reaction was that elegies can't be written soon enough for some of those knuckleheads.

But this was wishful thinking and thus of no practical use. He had never been good at arguing, let alone winning an argument. He left all that to those slicker of tongue and quicker on the draw than he. He supposed this could be construed as cowardice, but it had more to do with the fact that when it came to debate, he was like a guy who shows up at a machine gun fight with a single-shot muzzle-loader; he blew his wad early, likely missed the mark, and by the time he reloaded the war was over. Meanwhile, odds were good he'd shot himself in the foot, which coincidentally enough was lodged in his own mouth. Not the kind of warrior you want leading the charge.

He had read once that unity was utterly dependent on civility. The truth of this was never more evident and never more impotent. He imagined the civility quote as calligraphy inscribed on linen card stock, and the card a tattered little surrender hanky. He feared reliance on civility was improbably naïve. Also, as with many aphorisms, the whole works was open to interpretation, which spasmed right back to why he was no good at mixing it up in public and best off delivering soliloquies in a chicken coop.

But who am I helping, he thought, *if I dwell alone in gloom?*

His sense of self-loathing thus recharged, he headed back out into the snow. *Work it off,* he thought. Wading down to the brown pole barn where the heaters remained from the last go-round, he split the last of his kerosene between them and set both to a full roar. When he stepped back outside the snowflakes were still coming steadily, stirred now with a touch of wind.

Shit, he had to get to town.

Chapter Six

He hadn't run the truck for what, a month? Two months? It sat beneath a lump of snow beside the old milkhouse. Took him an hour to dig it out. The driver's side weatherstripping was iced shut so he had to pry the door. It tore loose with a sound like Velcro. When he finally settled into the seat, he was soaked with sweat. He twisted the key. Nothing happened. Dead battery.

He yanked his cap and sat there a moment, steam curling off his scalp. Here was the subtle evil of winter: not avalanches, not blinding blizzards, not freezing to death, just the damn drag on the day. Winter slows everything down. Every move. Every trip. Every chore. You can't just do things. You gotta gather your gear. Dress with intent. Double your socks. Triple your layers. Tuck things in or over, tug them up or cinch them down, do what it takes to keep the cold, snow, and melt from reaching your skin. Then you're so swaddled, you do any work at all you become your own sauna. And the second you slow down, you ice up.

The truck battery shits the bed in summer, you grab the nearest vehicle, hook up the jumper cables, give 'er a crank, and be on your way. Now even as he sat there, the windows had fogged up and frosted over on the inside from his breath and sweat. Her car was in the garage right across the yard with a battery fresh last fall, but it'd take him two more hours to shovel a lane from there to here and get it close enough for the cables to reach. The backhoe and dump truck were down in the red pole barn, busted down and out of the running, and who knew the state of their batteries after all the disuse. He considered starting the bulldozer, but once again that would require preheating and a prayer. In the end he figured the quickest solution was to trade out the truck battery for the car battery.

He trudged down to the red pole barn for the wrenches, then back up to the garage, then back to the pole barn because he forgot he needed a screwdriver, then back down again because he brought the metric wrench set when he needed standard, and then yet again for a Vise Grips and some cursing because one of the terminal clamps stripped out, but finally he tightened the last nut. The truck ground and ground, then shuddered to life. He left it running with the defroster on blast while he returned the tools, put the truck battery on trickle charge, and collected his kerosene containers.

The whole episode left him testy. As he heaved himself in behind the wheel, he shook his head. What was he upset about? It wasn't like he was late for an appointment. Or had to hit some deadline. Then he looked through the falling snow to the pole barns where the accumulation was deepening.

Well, a little deadline.

He clunked the truck into four-wheel-drive and surveyed the scene. Nothing but uncut white. It had always been one of his favorite things, plowing out that first run. Closest you could get in this day and age to striking out for the territories like in the cowboy books. It would be tough going, but because the driveway followed the ridge and cut through trees, it didn't collect snow like the space between the pole barns.

He dropped the plow, gunned the engine, and barged forward. A plume of snow exploded off the blade and curled through the air. Having lain so long, the snow had packed and settled, and the truck was laboring. He stuffed the accelerator to the floor and let it roar.

He hit a particularly solid drift, and snow billowed backward and into the windshield. The defroster was blowing hot, and the snow clung like paste to the glass. Running blind, he switched the wipers on, and they swept the slush aside. It was a moment of literal clarity, and he reveled in the beauty of the laden boughs overhanging the unsullied lane before him. Another drift, another blinding burst of white, and soon the wipers began to clack-clack, a sign they were getting gobbed with ice. It'd get to where they looked like one of those rock sugar lollipops. He lowered the window and reached around the door post, snatching at the wiper when it reached the end of its arc, snapping it against the glass to break loose the frozen slush.

He was nearly to the mailbox now. By reflex he veered leftward to check the contents, then recalled he had stopped the mail two weeks after she died. Called and told the postmaster he and the wife were taking another trip to Hawaii. It was an exhilarating lie and utterly out of character.

He broke through to the county road, raised the plow, and in his first moment off the farm since her death, felt afloat and untethered, as if he had been cut loose in space. Rather than drive, he sat idled on the centerline.

Back in his bachelor days, he dreamed of running country roads in a pickup truck with a wife slid over and sitting beside him. Indeed, early in the marriage, they found time now and then to do just that. By the time the barn burned, it was a rare and usually inadvertent occurrence, usually secondary to picking up feed or making a parts run; after the baby died it didn't happen at all. Now he was driving off the farm, and her body was back there on the porch. What if someone showed up while he was gone? He had nothing to hide, and never had, but at this point no explanation would be acceptable. He imagined having to stand there while some official ticked through a checklist, asking questions and taking notes. He couldn't explain himself. He was *done* explaining himself. Unless you had money or power, nothing was ever definitively solved. More than once lately when he stared at the snow, the phrase that came unbidden to mind was "clean slate." He'd take it as long as he could get it. He shifted the truck out of four-wheel drive and pressed the accelerator.

The county road followed the wide curve of the same ridge that passed through his farm. The landscape was mostly a checkerboard of open fields interspersed with woodlots and here and there a homestead. In these parts it was either trailer houses or mini-mansions and very little in between. He drove two miles before he encountered another vehicle, a black SUV that turned off the road before he met it and made its way up a snaking driveway to a house five times the size of his. A pair of software engineers, Harold recalled. They had hired him to dig their septic, although the arrangements had been made through a third-party property manager. It was odd to see a neatly plowed driveway, odd to see the automatic garage door rising as the SUV approached it. He felt like a man emerging from quarantine to find he had been the only one quarantining.

Another few miles, and the houses grew more prevalent. The farther he drove, the denser the developments. On certain overcast nights, he could see the glow of what was once the distant city. He had resented the encroachment even as he made his living moving dirt for those doing the developing. It was an old story. Go tell it to the Ojibwe.

At the farm store he arranged his kerosene receptacles in a row beside the pump. He had just begun filling the first when a slim fellow in a Subaru and a boutique earflapper cap rolled up, stepped out with a miniature blue canister, fidgeted impatiently, then spoke.

"What's all the kerosene for?"

Harold explained.

"Heaters going all night long?" said the man. "Gotta be hell on the environment. Whyn't you use a roof rake?"

"Because that would be like mowing a football field with a nose hair trimmer," said Harold in monotone. "Or the sweet little tweezers you use to do your eyebrows."

The blow failed to register.

"Yeah but all that fuel…"

Harold said no more. Just locked eyes with the man as the kerosene flowed. It was a dead calm stare. Not crazy-eyed, not frowny, just straight, solid, and direct as parallel steel rods. Five seconds in, the man dove back into his Subaru and sat cradling his canister. When his last can was topped, Harold re-racked the nozzle then took his sweet time re-capping each container and placing it neatly into the truck bed. When he finally drove away, he watched in his rearview mirror. The man remained in his car until Harold was clear of the lot and well down the frontage road. Harold smiled. Now and then you won one.

At the stop sign, he sat and let his right-turn signal click. The snow was falling unabated.

That coffee. How fine it would taste against this wintered up world.

But the pole barn roofs—they were probably groaning. And the heaters burning vapors.

He killed the blinker. Then flicked it to the left.

He wouldn't stay. He'd get the coffee to go. Had to, or he'd have two flat pole barns.

You don't know if she's even gonna be there.

JerLuna was at the door, flipping the sign to "CLOSED."

"Sunday," she said. "We close at four." But she held the door open. "I'll get you one to go."

He'd had no idea what day it was.

"Well, I…"

"C'mon," she said. He stepped through, and she locked the door behind him.

He wondered if she remembered him. Unlikely. He'd only been there once, and that was a while back. And despite his potentially memorable bumbling, he likely wasn't the only square who stumbled into the place hunting coffee only to realize he was better suited for self-serve from the gas station hot-pot.

Behind the bar, she unsleeved a large to-go cup, filled it, and placed it before him.

"Any food?"

"Oh, I don't wanna…"

"Chix Luv It, right?" She was smiling more than a little wickedly.

He should have known. Bartenders and baristas. Know you for your order.

"You tip low, then high."

Know you for your order, remember you for your tip.

"Yah, I guess." He blushed and looked at the bar tiles.

She giggled. "No worries. I gotcha. Have a seat."

It was odd to be the only customer in the place. The stillness of it. Even humans sitting still and staring at screens generate energy. The silence amplified the sound of her fixing his food. From his barstool he couldn't see her.

He reached over and punched the button on her phone. The screen lit up. Her and the little boy. Just the two of them. He jerked his finger back like the phone was hotwired to an electric fence, hoping against hope it would go dark before she brought his food. Just as she re-emerged, it faded to black.

"You're not the first person to wander in here and freeze up after three steps. It ain't for everyone."

"Oh, I didn't…"

"It's fine. You weren't expecting what you found. Then you carried on. Frankly, you don't strike me as someone who's comfortable in *any* public space."

"Pretty much."

"And yet here you are."

"Well…I just wondered…I knew…the coffee was good…last time I was in here it seemed like…" He trailed off, looking at her.

"Seemed like everything was going to shit?"

"Seemed to be leaning that way."

"You were eavesdropping on me that day."

He studied the tiles again.

"Update: everything that was *going* to shit, has *went* to shit."

Suddenly she was weeping. He reached toward her shoulder and then pulled back, having no idea what was appropriate.

The story poured out between ragged breaths. It began when Jer-Luna's longtime partner announced she was leaving. "We coulda been married, but we weren't," said JerLuna. "We shared everything. Now she *left* me with everything. Which is worse than nothing." She wiped her eyes and looked around the coffee shop. "This place kept us in rent but barely, and it took everything and every moment the two of us had to keep it going. Now she's gone. It's just me and Sam."

He felt the heat of the coffee through the paper cup. Outside it was nearly dark. Snowflakes coursed through the streetlight beam.

"I can't do it alone. She's off to Minneapolis with a fresh piece. Now I'm just another single mom with a shitty-ass car and no daycare. *Fierce*, my ass."

He put his hand atop hers and immediately jerked it back like he had touched the torpedo heater.

"Moot point, Sparky," said JerLuna with a half giggle, rolling her reddened eyes and blowing her nose on a napkin.

"I know, I know, I didn't mean it as…I don't…I know you're…I mean I'm *married*." His entire head had broken out in sweat.

"Tell me about your wife."

"She, ah."

"How long you been married?"

In blind panic, he tried to do the math.

"Dude, you shouldn't have to do the math."

"I'm a bad husband."

"There are a lot of you."

"I mean, not bad, not like…I've never…I've always…" His heart was thudding.

"Screwed around? Not even what I was thinking," said JerLuna. She stood and began to wipe down the counter. "She work?"

"We had a farm. Have it. But farming… She works at the Dollar Store. *Worked*. She's been sick."

"I'm sorry to hear it."

After a pause, JerLuna said, "Kids?"

He stood and backed away from the counter. The urge to tell her everything was overpowering. Like standing at a railing, fighting the urge to jump.

"No." He gulped. It felt as though a snowball was wedged down his throat. "No kids."

"Well, pros and cons," said JerLuna. "But I'd throw myself in front of your snowplow to save my little guy. Honestly, he's the only thing that keeps me going right now. If I fail, I fail him." She teared up again.

"Where is he now?"

JerLuna stepped from behind the bar and nodded for him to follow, and he did, back past the tables and couches, then down a short hallway past the restrooms to a storage room. The door was ajar. The boy was asleep in a pile of blankets, just his face and curls visible. A clutter of coloring books and crayons surrounded him.

"I just wish…" whispered JerLuna, and then there was a *ding* from the kitchen.

"Oh shit, the sandwich," she said, and ran back to the front of the shop.

There was silence then, as he stared at the bundle on the floor, the blanket rising and falling. He knelt and listened. Soon he heard it, the breath passing in and out of the child, steady and soft. How briefly he had known that sound. He thought of the crick on his farm. What the water must sound like right now, flowing beneath the ice.

"Overtoasted!" said JerLuna, handing him the Chix Luv It in a box. He fumbled around for his money.

"Forget it," she said. "Coffee was gonna get dumped anyway, and seven bucks for a sandwich ain't gonna fix this mess. It was good to talk."

He picked up his coffee and started to leave, then stopped, then didn't know what to say.

"Yer fine," said JerLuna. "I gotta lock up."

Her car was parked beside his truck. There wasn't much visible beneath the snow. A fringe of rust. The rear passenger window replaced with plastic sheeting and duct tape. One missing hubcap. On closer inspection he noted the wheel missing a hubcap was a miniature spare.

There was rust around the lug nuts, indicating she'd been running that spare a while now. A hallmark sign of scraping by.

He was halfway through his sandwich and departing the city limits before he realized she was right at that moment sweeping the snow from her car, and it had never occurred to him to do it for her. He let off the gas, then realized it was pointless. He turned on to the county road, following his headlights through an infinite tunnel of illuminated snowflakes. This vision and the silence of the cab amplified the sense of dislocation precipitated by the coffee shop stop. He switched the radio on.

He used to sing along with the country music oldie station in his pickup truck, but after the baby died every lyric was razor wire. You couldn't listen without slicing yourself. The dumbest song, the sweetest song, each laced his gut with lead. Music is the universal language, they say, but it never found a way to speak any sense into losing that little bundle. God never gives us more than we can handle, said a lady at the funeral, but any given sixty seconds of the daily news belies that, and he wondered if it was possible to convey how it felt to be strafed by "You Are My Sunshine" emanating from the supermarket ceiling speakers a month after buying your first and last pack of diapers.

Nowadays he would spin through the dial less to listen and more as a listless rebellion against instant gratification. He had long ago lost the vinegar required to advocate for or against any particular song or genre. Even the talk radio hosts and all their disingenuous barking failed to piss him off anymore. *Radio knobs*, he thought. Not that anyone under fifty would get that joke.

He spun down the dial and back again. The last time a song held his attention, it was "Mercury in Retrograde" by Sturgill Simpson. It floated through his pickup truck radio from the college station that'd come in now and then if the weather was right. The lyrics told a story a million miles removed from his life but dead center to his existence. Simpson sang like he was using his middle finger for a microphone. Harold listened, and it felt like his heart was forming a fist. His favorite lyric came tagged on the end of the third verse: *Sorry boys, the bus is plumb full.*

God, how he wanted to spit that line at the world and every idiot in it.

In his absence the driveway had infilled. He dropped the blade and roared forward. Upon reaching the house he was tempted to blast all the way down to the pole barns, but the snow down there was deep and dense...if he stuck the truck in the swale it'd be lodged 'til spring.

Instead he donned his snowshoes and bulled down to the brown pole barn with a can of kerosene in each hand. By the time he pushed through the door he was sweaty and blown. Both heaters were drained and cold. *Dammit, I shoulda come straight back home.* The interior was dead quiet; when he tipped the kerosene can, he could hear every slurp and gurgle. He looked to the rafters and imagined the weight above him and more falling every minute. He wondered if he'd pay a price for stopping at the coffee shop. When the heaters were lit he fought his way back to the house, set his alarm for 2 a.m., slept until it buzzed, and refueled the heaters again. Playing the flashlight over the roof, he saw it was still covered in snow, but he could hear melt running off the eaves, and a fissure had opened at the peak. The mass was inching free.

Returning to the house he stoked the wood stove, then rather than bedding down he left the firebox door ajar, backed to the couch, wrapped himself in blankets, and stared into the flames. His breathing slowed, his eyes fell out of focus. The fire blurred to a pulsing blob. In this state, he was still capable of peace. Inner peace, peace of mind. Peace of muscle and bone. Everything in him stilled but his heart, and even that floating more than beating.

He recalled how he would find her at dawn cross-legged on her yoga mat and supposed she would have said he wasn't staring, he was meditating. He supposed it didn't matter. He just knew the stillness left him feeling simultaneously stone solid and light as air. When he hunkered like this, he invariably realized all it was he was hiding from. Or hidden from. Or spared. That the globe all around him was boiling and jagged, and he had no more defense against fate than a slug in a salt factory, but somehow he had been allowed this cocooned moment. He figured you absorbed this sort of thing as long as it was given. The key was to remark it. To acknowledge it. He sometimes thought this would be the best way to die: the body at painless stasis, hovering within gravity, everything at equilibrium. Then just fade.

Three or four times a year, she'd ask him to join her in a morning meditation. Just five minutes. He never had. Every dawn he woke slow-burning to get at the work of the day. To shoulder the load like it was the cross. In retrospect, he was an ass.

He had to take a leak. *Thus concludes our meditation,* he thought. Stepping outside, he peed, the porch light illuminating the steam curling off his stream. He hadn't tried to write his name in the snow since his teens, but there was still a low-level fascination in the way the urine pierced the snow like a plasma cutter through steel, inscribing a line whichever way he directed it. Exposed in the cold he felt less like he was pointing a nozzle than nudging an acorn, so he didn't fool around, just peed straight and contented himself with watching the round hole form and expand, then slowly tail off toward his toes.

Just as the last drop fell, there arose from behind the spruce a whoosh followed by thuds.

The brown pole barn.

Calving its snow load.

He whooped right out loud.

Sure enough, when he bundled up and snowshoed down there, the flashlight shone on a slick roof. Unfortunately the snow itself hadn't stopped, so he immediately began the process of transferring the heaters back to the red pole barn.

In minutes he was raging. The snow was so deep and the heater so ungainly, he could only yank it ahead a few feet at a time. He was huffing and puffing like it was dog days of August at high school football practice and he was lunging at a blocking sled. A snowshoe detached, and he pitched face first into a drift.

Recovering his feet, he bent to fix his snowshoe and lost his balance, this time twisting an ankle as he toppled. He screamed into the snow, then rolled to his back, gasping with his cap askew. To calm himself, he focused on the ache of the snow melting against his skull.

Rage had infected him ever since the baby died. A seething core of suppressed fury. The slightest prick and it spit black acid. Once he clenched his teeth so hard he cracked a molar. Another time he drove his fist into a six-by-six. He felt his knuckle split, and the blood flow. When the adrenaline receded he felt refreshed, as if his arteries had been blown clean.

There was nothing refreshing in humping these heaters. But god-dammit, he stuck with it. He guessed he was bred to. *Work harder* was the answer to everything. He fixed his snowshoe and went back to dragging the heater through the drifts, foot-by-foot, until with a final lurch and curse he yanked it through the door. He stood for a moment, breathing hard, sweat running down his neck. Then he clomped back after the second heater. For all his reading, he'd never made it through *Moby Dick*, but he figured he was going full Ahab. And to think an hour ago he was congratulating himself on his ability to meditate.

When the heaters were set and lit yet again, he returned to the house only to discover he had never closed the wood stove door, and the smoke detector was squealing. Standing on a kitchen chair, he un-twisted it from the mount, dropped it to the floor, jumped off boot-heels-first, and smashed it to bits.

When his alarm sounded beside the bed, the sky was graying up and the snow had stopped. *Paused, more likely*, he thought. Making his way down to refuel the heaters, he looked with hope for the telltale roofline crack, but there was no break. And although the snow had stopped falling, he'd never seen it stacked so high. *You and yer god-damn coffee break. If that thing goes down, it's 'cause you was someplace you had no reason to be.*

The heaters replenished, he dug his daily path to the chicken coop. For breakfast he scrambled five eggs right out of his pocket and ate baked beans from the can. After the long interrupted night and now the food, he longed to collapse and sleep, but the last refill had drained the second of the two kerosene containers he'd taken down the night before. He'd have to lug a fresh one from the truck.

Goddammit, he thought, as he stared downslope to the pole barn, snowshoes dangling from his hand. *I ain't draggin' my ass down through all that again.* He started the truck, let it warm, then revved it.

Damn the torpedoes time, he thought. He checked that it was in four-wheel-drive, backed up the driveway twenty yards or so, and shifted into first gear. Then he tromped the gas and dropped the blade.

The snow burst from the blade. He swung leftward off the ridge and dove toward the pole barns. He imagined himself piloting a bomber. Still picking up speed, he punched the clutch and went for second gear. It was a dumb mistake he regretted immediately. In the very instant the transmission was disengaged, he cleared the spruce line and hit the chest-deep hard-packed snow accumulated in the swale. It was as if he had rammed a concrete wall. The angle of the blade at impact levered the rear end of the truck sideways and his head smacked the window. He tried reverse, but even in four-wheel drive the wheels just spun, the blade set like an anchor, and the tailgate packed against a wall of snow. He shifted back to first, tried to push forward, and didn't make it an inch. He felt his gut sink and the flop sweat rise.

He had *known* better.

"You fucking IDIOT!" he roared. Pushing the accelerator flat to the floor, he let the engine scream. All four wheels spun and chattered, the rubber lugs failing to grab but setting the cab to jouncing as if he were crossing a rock patch. "Fuck, fuck, fuck!" he screamed, his foot jammed downward so hard his ass was levering right up off the seat. Even as he recognized the madness in this, he felt as if the whirling engine was a vortex drawing poison off his soul. Now he could smell hot rubber as the tires melted through the pack snow and ice down to the frozen gravel, but still the truck did not budge, and then the vibration of the chassis shifted to something more centered and solid and the motor slid to a higher pitch, and then there was an explosive *crack-BAM*, a flush of oily smoke farted out from beneath the hood, and then nothing but the cooling tick of the cracked engine block.

He sat there until the windshield fogged and froze. Finally, unable to open his door, he reached beneath the seat, drew out a tire iron and drove it through the window, stirred the residual glass clear, and crawled out. Reaching into the bed, he pulled out a kerosene can and fought his way to the pole barn where he refilled and restarted the heaters as if the truck trouble hadn't happened. It struck him that his detachment was more unnatural than his rage.

When he topped the fuel at noon, the snow mass had finally cracked. An hour later it had slipped a hands-breadth and was curling over the eaves, but it hadn't broken loose. By midafternoon the wind was up and driving fine, icy bits of snow that stung against his cheeks. When he fought his way back up out of the swale after his 10 p.m. refueling trip, he was leaning into a full-on blizzard. He didn't bother to play the flashlight beam over the roof. He didn't want to know. He couldn't imagine the structure surviving this.

The wood stove was gone to embers so he laid in some kindling, Lincoln-logged some bigger chunks atop it, set the draft wide open, and sat on the couch to watch until it caught. He could hear the gusting wind, the tick of snow flung against the windows, and imagined the hard-earned gap filling with snow, the rooftop sheet cake deepening and the melt slowing as the temperature fell.

He'd set the alarm for 2 a.m. again. Keep the heaters cranking all night long. He leaned his head back, staring as thin flames rose around the kindling.

He was dead asleep when he startled awake to a crack the likes of which he hadn't heard since lightning split the giant yard pine.

Then a fireworks string of them and the screech of rending tin.

Then *whomp*.

The fire was back to embers. He drew the blankets around him and slept again.

Chapter Seven

When he woke the firebox was cold. The outside world was dead still. He strapped into his snowshoes and made his way down past the marooned plow truck, now just a rooftop amidst the drifts.

Three of the red pole barn walls still stood. The fourth swooned inward, providing a view to the remains of the roof. It lay inverted and crumpled, a snow bowl bristling with splintered trusses. The force of the expelled air had blown scraps of black tar paper and pink insulation outward, forming a confetti blast zone. A strip of bright blue tarp hung from the branches of a leafless boxelder; a nearby stretch of fence was dammed with sheets of paper and feed bags.

The access door hung from a single hinge. He knelt down and peered within. There was little to see. A scattering of wrenches from a toppled tool cart. A pair of wooden handles, flat to the ground, the wheelbarrow to which they were attached buried in the crush. The portable air compressor, sitting at a cant, one wheel snapped off from the weight of debris covering it. He always kept the compressor near the door so if a tire went low, he could drive up and run the hose out the door. He entertained a brief cartoony vision of reinflating the building.

His next inclination was to light a match. Burn the whole works. The scent of kerosene was in the air, meaning the heaters were still running when the roof went down, and whatever fuel was in them had likely been expelled as they were crushed. The arson option wasn't as ridiculous as the re-inflation fantasy, but it didn't hold up any better under scrutiny. After all the combustibles went up you'd still have a pile of scorched tin and tools and machinery. And the smoke—rubber tires, motor oil, treated wood—the black cloud would boil straight up, hit a thermal layer, then slide flatly downwind along the ridge, visible for miles. Someone would call the fire department or send the sheriff or just get nosy.

No, he thought. *No.* He realized his heart was racing.

The insurance guy. He should call the insurance guy. It wasn't so much a thought as a reflex.

Of course not. Different smoke, same fire.

The chickens. I haven't done the chicken chores. With relief he turned to the solid distraction of it.

It took him an hour to shovel through. He welcomed the exertion, and staring back up the clean-cut path to the house, he felt relief at the imposition of this slender strip of order.

There was a rumble from the Jones place. He moved forward for a look. A bulldozer, beetling back and forth, pushing the collapsed loafing barn into a pile. A large yellow excavator fitted with pincers, swinging to and fro, depositing the remnants in a fleet of dump trucks that came and went.

He ate his eggs and beans, then took a mug of tea to the porch and surveyed his remaining outbuildings. The garage, the granary, the corn cribs, the old milkhouse, the machine shed, and the brown pole barn—still standing but probably bound to collapse at the next snowfall now that his torpedo heaters were snuffed for good amongst the remains of the red pole barn. How neat the other structures appeared, arranged about the property against the white backdrop. He knew better, of course. Each was crammed with junk. Storehouses of dead ends. Entropy by the boxful. *How much stuff do we keep in our lives under the assumption we will use it again,* he wondered. He had never sold off love and affection, but he might as well have. He imagined it boxed up and stuck on a folding table, tagged with a masking tape price tag, twenty-five cents maybe, scribbled with a Sharpie.

He supposed if she was alive and pressed on the question she'd say their love had yielded diminishing returns. No, something steeper than that, whatever's the opposite of compounding interest. *Exsanguinating* interest, maybe. You started out storing memories in a treasure chest; in the end it was just another dumpster.

He looked at the buildings again, envisioning every abandoned, tumbled, neglected, unrepaired outdated object represented, and felt revulsion. What would it be like to start over? To see life laid out before you as clean and white as a winter hayfield? This was the true power of the snow. Its ability to obscure. To create the appearance of purification. For all he fought the snow, for all the shoveling, all the maddening trudging, all the impotent raging, he feared much more the melt. At least in deep freeze there was solidity. Misery in stasis rather than misery multiplying. No surprises.

The contents of the fallen pole barn—of every building on this place, for that matter—were emblematic of survival, toil, and sentimentality. He had let it all collect based on some hazy hunch that one day the work would be done and the past could be reassembled or at least sorted. Now he felt nothing but the dead weight of it.

How much of his dark mental meandering had seeped into her? All those times when he couldn't even bring himself to be borderline pleasant. And transposing the amoral misbehavior of outsiders into impatience with the woman he'd loved? Who had loved *him*? What the hell sort of inorganic chemistry equation was that? He was the insufferable "longing man." What good was exploring your inner dimensions if you kept them walled off from the person in your bed? *In short, son,* he thought, *you are a narcissist and the best thing you can do is clear off and clear out.*

He looked to his right, to her body in the blankets. Then back to the concave pole barn, the split tin, the bits of color snagged in the surrounding brush.

There's your terror, he thought. *Everything busted out into the wide open.*

Back in the house he stared at his collection of books, as if there was anything of help in them. *Philosophize yer way outta this,* he thought.

He hauled in some firewood. He sat on the couch. He had no idea what to do next. The torpedo heaters had been his one driving purpose, and now they were junk.

At dusk he walked down for another look at the Jones place. The trucks, excavator, and dozer were gone. The spot where the building had stood was a flat smear of brown.

Chapter Eight

That night the temperature plummeted, freeze-drying the air. At first light every tree branch, every blackberry cane, every stick and stem was a hoarfrost wand. The sky was clear, the air was still, and sunlight splintered every which way. When the chicken chores were complete, he strapped into his snowshoes and set out downrange, toward the back forty.

The snow was pure and soft and clean and sugar-sifty and utterly untracked. The sound of his steps were like a feather drawn through sand. His breath rolled out before him in a gossamer purl. He noted his heart pumping with exertion rather than madness or panic, and for the first time since the day she died, his subconscious fed him a stream of happy associations. Specifically, him as a child: scrubbing his sled runners with a block of candle wax; the feel of his belly pressed against the wooden slats of the sled deck as he beamed red-cheeked and runny-nosed into the onrushing wind; later, cider with a cinnamon stick; his mother, tucking the blanket about him on the couch, boiling water, bringing him crackers and Cup-a-Soup.

He reached up and flicked a popple branch. The frost dislodged, drifting down to dust his boot toes like a scattering of instant potato flakes. Again he thought of his mother and the box of Hungry Jack she stored in the corner cupboard of her kitchen, the one at floor level, to the left of the sink. The image came to him like a snapshot taken from the perspective of a preschooler. A watery dish of Hungry Jack had been among his favorite things because his mother made up for the thinness with plenty of butter.

Bad food, he thought. *Good memories*. He wished he had some Hungry Jack right now. His last few potatoes were in a box in the basement, sprouting and going soft.

Potato-flake snow, he mouthed to himself, pretending for a moment he was a poet. He recalled reading somewhere that the old saw about Eskimos having 100 words for snow was—as with many old saws—bullshit. The lodestones of our lives are in fact shifty and adrift. The same article detailed questions and contentions over the term Eskimo itself. He'd resolved to switch to Inuit, but memories and reflex are slow to reform.

He moved on, then knelt to inspect a goldenrod gall. It rode frosted on its stalk, an encrusted scepter. He found the hole where a chickadee had bored in for the larva. The ones the birds missed would survive to spring because their cells were laced with natural antifreeze. A marvel. And how did the novice chickadee know to peck its first gall? Nature was a mind-bender. He was still on his knees and for reasons he could not explain raised his face and stared at the sun. When he looked away the image hung on his retinas like a radioactive plum. He turned his eyes left, then right, the scorch following at a lag.

Lately every retrospection slid into acidity. Or rancidity. He'd recall the smell of warm cows in winter, of slatted sunlight through the haymow siding, the whitewash peeling, the soft clink of the stanchion chains, and even though he had experienced them firsthand, he now felt them as failed mythology. The memories that once soothed him had lost their solace.

He assumed this was due to having been raised in decency, then watching so many debased graspers win. You saw a satisfied smile on the face of some soulless shyster, and you questioned the idiocy of naïve striving. You felt like a kid in hand-me-down Sunday clothes with a single hard-earned nickel, trying to buy gum drops at a strip club.

He had been seduced by bitterness and was circling cynicism but held fast against nihilism. You couldn't do that to other people. To the good people. The gentle people. The helpless. He fantasized sometimes about selling the farm and donating all the money to some just cause. He hadn't the caliber to fight on the front lines. He wasn't fit for the bleeding edge. But he also lately realized that seething in silence from the safety of the sidelines was little more than petulance as privilege.

With a start, he realized he was still kneeling. Shaking his head as if he'd had his bell rung, he stood and looked around like a boxer searching for his corner. His propensity for mental steeplechases was becoming pathological. Round and round, hopping the same hurdles while standing still.

He clomped clear out to the back forty, back to the barbed wire where he had cursed and wept the day he sold the beef cows. It seemed another lifetime ago, a chronologic cliché if ever there was one. He breathed deeply and held it. Focused on the stillness. The stillness, and the bright silence. The air all oxygen and clarity. He wondered if souls were real, and if so, did his wife see him down here, a poisonous dot in the infinite white?

Was there any way to feel shame without it presenting as an excuse? What good is shame after the fact? When you can't make it right? It was a true mystery how she died, but there was no mystery in the fact of him having given her no happiness in the time prior. What rank evil was it to know yourself this well and do nothing to change? Every gentle thought he had about her now was nothing less than self-serving mitigation. No matter how deep his regret, no matter how sincere his repentance, he remained convicted. Not one little electron flash of it brought any light at all to the darkness of their final years. The moment she died, the moment he could no longer atone, his every breath was sour with self-justification.

His book-reading, his doofy philosophizing, these amounted to little more than a grandiose attempt at mythologizing shittiness. Sometimes, when she was still alive, even after things were bad, he would be at work in the woods or back forty and find himself longing for her as in the early days. Eventually it occurred to him that he only ever missed her from a distance.

Well it was nothing but distance now.

Six snowmobiles shot over the rise and buzz-sawed his reverie to bits. Wallowing in his navel, he hadn't registered their muffled whine. Now here they came, tearing full throttle up the valley, the garish suits and helmets and engine cowlings as jarring as spring breakers stampeding a meditation session. The sleds shot past like warplanes on a strafing run, just downhill from where he stood. Of course the riders had no idea he was there. They cut across a corner of his property and in seconds were gone, the trailing snow cloud settling, their tracks striping the snow like whip strokes.

He raised both hands toward the spot where they disappeared and shot a double bird. As he was wearing heavy leather chopper mitts, the effect was less than he hoped. He leaned over, tightened his snowshoes, and hiked homeward into the recovered silence. He was halfway back when the wind rose, freeing soft cyclones of frost. All around him the air sparkled, a crystalline spill.

Upon returning to the yard, he ran an extension cord to the bulldozer, plugged in the block heater, and attached a charger to the battery. It occurred to him that he hadn't paid his electric bill, but the power company was legally prevented from cutting the power until spring. He'd always paid every bill and disdained those who didn't. Paid them early in fact. *Who's a deadbeat now?* he thought.

The bulldozer would need a while to warm and charge. He took the time to pull the battery from the plow truck and put it back in her car. *Just in case*, he thought, although he came up short on what exactly that case might be.

Back at the dozer, he dug and swept the controls and cockpit clear, checked the oil and fuel and fluids then tried the starter. It ground strenuously, then the engine coughed and caught, the poorly combusted diesel rolling white then black from the stack. He let it sit at idle, the exhaust pipe flapper bouncing and rattling. He could hear the engine warming itself, becoming more efficient, smoothing out.

From the cockpit he surveyed the wreckage of the red pole barn. He had no plan, just a desire to act. There had been this feeling in him, this impatience, and it had been amplified by the erasure of the Jones' loafing barn. He didn't have the resources of the Jones boys—he had neither the means nor the desire to invite or hire help in the disposal of what after all was hard evidence of his own deterioration. What he did have was a bulldozer and over by the granary, a big tank of diesel fuel.

Already you are overthinking, he thought, and pushed the hand clutch forward. The tracks were iced up and broke free with a crack, then the dozer puttered ahead, cleats clanking, blading the snow aside like nothing. Working the clutch and brake system he spun the dozer around and cut a half-circle until he was bearing down on the near corner of the fallen pole barn. He bumped the throttle, then bumped it again. He eased forward until the blade was pressed into the tin, then pushed forward. The cleats chattered for a moment, then the corner pole snapped, taking half of the standing wall with it. Harold bumped the throttle again and watched with relish as the exhaust pipe rolled coal, the black plume shooting skyward as the sheet metal screeched and tore.

He dozed the length of the building, then just kept going, across the ridge until he came to the lip of the ravine and sent the trash tumbling over the snowy brink. Reversing course, he took another swipe. And then another. With each pass he exposed more and more of the pole barn contents. A jumble of old memories and the recent past: a recliner she'd hoped to reupholster, a splintered set of antique wooden wagon wheels he'd promised to mount on the granary as decoration, the rusted-out grain cart he'd always intended to patch.

He could only push so much per pass. The excess spilled around the sides of the blade. But he had all the time in the world. He pushed, reversed, then pushed again. At one point the blade gouged through the snow and into the topsoil. He stopped the dozer and studied the deep brown stripe scoring the white. You get this deeply into winter, you sustain snowfall at these record levels, when the blade skins up a little color, you have this moment of imminent recollection where you realize you *forgot* about dirt. Or even more startlingly, the bright green skid mark tracking back to a clump of frozen grass rolled up in a lump of ice, looking rare as a prehistoric bug in amber.

He climbed down, pulled off one glove, and picked up a grassy clod. Held it to his nose, and the scent rose with the heat of his palm. Dew and birdsong. Springtime. Her. Them. Hand-in-hand. Those early days. There was the urge to fling the clod as far as he could. Instead he dropped it, remounted, and goosed the throttle.

As with his snow shoveling, he tried to keep the bulldozing neat. Squared up the edges. He wondered if this compulsion tied to a time in his youth when he passed through a period of obsessive-compulsive behavior. He'd lay out his clothes on the bed, everything flat and smoothed and no edge touching another edge. He couldn't dress himself until he'd done it. Same with the contents of his backpack. Everything arranged atop the mattress, then re-packed. During this same stretch, he couldn't walk around the left side of anything; it always had to be the right side. He'd tap his toothbrush on the sink exactly four times in a pattern—*rat-tatta-tat*—before returning it to the holder. Eventually these compulsions passed. He didn't recall "working through" it or making any intentional decision to stop. He just phased out of it. The only residual effect was an understanding of those who truly suffered from more intractable, long-term disorders. He'd remember how carefully he smoothed his socks in alignment and didn't think these people were being silly.

In short, shoving everything into the ravine was soothing. When the poles snapped off at ground level, it bugged him a bit to think of the residual stubs beneath the surface, an imperfection. But then his face twisted into a smirk as he figured imperfection below the surface was the moral to this whole damn story. Exhibit A, the precisely shoveled path leading to his hovel house.

The light was fading, and he was hungry. *One more pass,* he thought, and drove the dozer forward. The blade hooked a cardboard box and spun it sideways. PHOTO ALBUMS it said on the side. He stopped the dozer and stared at the box. *You're a fool to open it,* he thought. *And a coward not to.*

He dismounted, unpocketed his jackknife, slit the packing tape, and raised the flaps, revealing an album embossed with silver scrollery: *WEDDING.* He flipped it open. There was just one photograph on the first page, the standard headshot portrait, the two of them leaning into each other but looking at the camera, a stiff simulacrum of what he'd actually been feeling that day: certainty, quiet happiness, gratitude that somehow he'd found her and she him.

The next couple of pages were from their early dating days. The two of them leaning against the farm truck when it was new. He remembered the first time she helped him load it with hay, the way she swung and pitched the bales. The two of them standing on the walkway of the barn, cow butts in the frame to either side, him with his arm around her, grinning like a booted doofus.

It had been so long since he had felt purely happy he wasn't certain it had ever occurred, despite this photographic evidence. Every now and then, at the scent of melting ice, or the call of a bird, or the stillness of a dirt road, he'd catch some reminiscent tug, some faint light note that resonated like a steel guitar string plucked just once then instantly dampened by the heel of an invisible hand. It was as if his head remembered love but his heart could not. He withdrew the photo of them in the barn and placed it in his pocket, then turned the page. A single loose Polaroid flittered to the snow: the baby, red-faced and hospital swaddled.

He slapped the album shut, dropped it in the box, turned the baby picture face-down atop it, and interlocked the box flaps. He caught a whiff of kerosene and for a split second considered setting the box afire. An overwhelming sacrilege. Or a necessary exorcism. He toed the box back before the blade, climbed aboard the dozer, reached for the throttle, then folded his arms across the dashboard, dropped his head, and wept.

When he raised his eyes, the sun had sunk, leaving a pale orange rim at the horizon. He refueled, then shut the dozer down and plugged it in so it would start come morning. Then he retrieved the box of photos, carried it to the porch, and placed it beside her blanketed body.

He had the vague idea that come spring he'd bury her with the pictures. As if for all the shit and sadness somehow this would put a ribbon on it. And hell, why wait until spring? The dozer had power aplenty to bust the frost. But the idea of putting her into frozen ground made him recoil. He knew this was irrational, but that was irrelevant. The baby was buried in the county cemetery several miles away. He wanted them together. He'd backed himself into a corner that would never allow that now. Burying her here with that picture seemed the only way to even things up.

He sensed he was coming unglued. Delaminating. Closing his eyes for a moment, he caught a vision of himself as a puppet dangling, his strings fraying. He wondered how long he could forestall his own collapse.

Back in the house he pulled the photo of the two of them grinning in the barn from his pocket and propped it on the nightstand beside the bed.

That night he slept deeply without dreaming.

Chapter Nine

By noon the next day he shoved the last of the red pole barn and its contents into the ravine. It took him a while to shift the bigger stuff. The dump truck and the equipment trailer kept rolling and twisting and sliding sideways off the blade, but he came at them again and again, coaxing them side to side, working them like a slow-motion herding dog. When the last bit tumbled from sight, he spent an hour smoothing the scene, plowing back and forth so the scraped area was neatly cleaned and uniformly lined with cleat tracks. He sat the dozer at idle and surveyed the scene for a good long time, same as when he finished stacking wood, or hay bales, or shoveling the chicken coop path, indulging an innate male desire to review and commemorate the completion of even the most basic task.

Then he spun the dozer and studied the brown pole barn. It was heavily snowcapped but still standing. He eased the machine forward and brought it to a stop with the blade an inch from the corrugated steel. The diesel held at a low rattle. He figured he should have felt like he was standing with his toes at the edge of a canyon, ready to leap. In fact the dozer seat felt like an easy chair. He considered the contents of the building before him. The side delivery hay rake with a cracked drive gear. The tractor-mounted corn picker, not good for much but scrap. The grain drill, tiny as a toy by today's agribusiness standards. The dusty twine rolls, the empty feed sacks, the jars and boxes of parts and mismatched screws and nuts and bolts and broken-handled rakes and rags and things he had bought at auctions decades ago and never touched again. He envisioned what it would take to get rid of it all, the sorting and rearranging and dump runs and then meeting with the auctioneer to go through every square foot so it could all be online in expandable thumbnails for people to study and appraise. *Strangers zooming in on my crap*, he thought.

And then the day itself: more strangers—and worse, neighbors—parking their trucks up and down the driveway, walking right onto the property, crisscrossing the yard with Styrofoam cups of coffee and a doughnut from the concessions trailer, the auctioneer yodeling along and calling out his name when it was time to give context to an object or verify when the head gasket had last been replaced on the Oliver, all eyes turning on him standing there, mortified in his coveralls, and he drove the throttle as far forward as it would go. Black smoke pumped out the straight stack in a velvet billow, the blade punched through the tin, the corner post cracked like a leg bone, the corrugated sheets screeched and popped their nail-head buttons, and he didn't let up until the side of that pole barn was gut-slit end-to-end.

Well, that's a damn start, he thought, and backed up for another pass.

He had to be careful. He wished he had one of those excavators like they used down there at the Jones place. Extend the arm, drag the roof and rafters down from a distance. The dozer limited his options. He couldn't just plow into the building and risk bringing it all down on his head. He was protected by roll bars and a steel roof, but let a splintered truss shish kebab him or a sheet of tin slash his neck, and the coyotes would find him bled out in the snow. Life had lost its zip, but he retained his dumb drive to finish the job. There was danger to what he was doing but not *much* danger. Furthermore, the power of danger lay in fear, and he'd pretty well been leached of fear. He wasn't hunting a bullet, but neither would he duck one.

He wondered as he worked another pass of trash toward the ravine what exactly *would* upset him at this point. Widen his eyes. Knock him off course. Or what his course even was. *In the course of human events*, he thought, by tangential reflex. It felt like something he'd learned in elementary school. Sure enough, he remembered, the Declaration of Independence. Perhaps these dozer trails were lines composing his own declaration of independence. *Ridiculous piffle*, he thought, rolling his eyes even though there was no one there to see it. *You are overwrought.* He pressed one finger against his nose and fired a snot rocket. It gobbed against the cleats and rode the track out of sight.

He pushed the load over the edge and while backing away, spotted the hatchet he'd used to break ice for the beef cows. In an instant he was overcome with longing for the moment he'd discovered the steel head, his present weathered form utterly inhabiting the memory of a little boy left to his own time and devices, a little boy with his mind so alive he could conjure overlapping legends of how that hatchet came to be there, never mind that some weary farmer simply discarded it. He dismounted the dozer, picked up the hatchet, and held it to his chest. *Maybe*, he thought. *Maybe.* He stood still a long moment then drew his arm back and flung the hatchet with all the force he could muster. Watched it fly end-over-end then tuck soundlessly into the snow far below. He liked to think of it suspended there. Encased in snowflakes, floating just above the ground, waiting to be lowered to the earth by thaw.

Once again he ran the dozer until dusk. He pulled up to the diesel tank and left the engine to cool at idle while he refueled. Half of the brown pole barn was swept away. It didn't seem odd now, it seemed like a job. It seemed a *relief.* There had been enough repressed panic. Enough stupid stoicism. He was letting go of everything, and it felt quietly, deeply satisfying. It was as if he had cleared his closets of every family heirloom, burned them in the hearth one by one, and rather than loss felt lightness. It was as if when the roof of that red pole barn fell in, his troubles rose out.

Later when he stepped off the porch to take a leak, the moon hung full and bright. The chicken coop was a dark cube against the lunarscape. While zipping he realized he hadn't collected the eggs. As he walked the path it occurred to him that there had been no snowfall since he started bulldozing. It seemed ages since he last shoveled.

When he cracked the coop door and the moonlight cut in, a couple of the birds shifted, and there were muted tut-tuts, but otherwise they stayed put. Once settled they tended to stay fixed as if hypnotized. Once he found a neat row of nine dead hens after a weasel slunk in and drank their blood one by one, each roosting patiently until it was her turn to die.

Been a while since I butchered a chicken, he thought, and for good reason: the last time he opened the chest freezer in the garage it was so empty it echoed. Back in the day this would have been unheard of. They always put up stores, canning and freezing, stocking the cellar with root vegetables, butchering the venison he took during hunting season, making their own sausage. The one thing they didn't eat was beef, as it was worth more on the trailer than in the freezer. The pantry, too, was developing an echo. He was pretty much down to canned beans.

So many autumn days spent in the steam of the kitchen, the stove overloaded, the countertops crowded with cutting boards and colanders and jars. In the early days there was here and there a sly pinch or nudge, maybe a break to run to the bedroom. One night they canned 'til sundown, and as she rinsed a saucepan in the sink he stood behind her and palmed her belly where the baby was growing. She told him once she had harbored visions of working in the garden with the baby asleep in a bassinet beneath the basswood tree that smelled so sweet three days a year. The way she spoke it was like a poem. After the baby died they worked in silence. This last fall they hadn't canned at all, he hadn't gone hunting, and it'd been years since they raised a pig.

So he was down to eggs and beans. Tempting as it was, if he started butchering chickens it'd be a cascade of diminishing returns. He felt around the laying boxes for the eggs and placed them in his coat pocket. Two of the nests were occupied. He slid his hand beneath the feathered warmth and fished the eggs out, neither bird protesting beyond a sleepy chirp.

When he stepped outside there was an explosion of huffing and snorting and dark figures scattering every which way. Deer. They'd surrounded the coop while he was inside, likely to paw around outside in hopes of finding a stray bit of straw. It was another sign that the snow was interfering with their foraging. Indeed, rather than fleeing fleetly, they were galumphing and humping through the snow, breaking trail with their briskets. He watched as they circled and reconvened, inky blots drawing back together until they were back to trail and flowing in a line.

Beneath the brightness of the moon, he followed them, wading until he hit the trough of their common tracks. The light was such that he could see the general shape of things, although in a color-blind way. The trail led through scrub and brush and into a pine copse so thick very little snow had fallen through to the understory, leaving instead a blanket of shed needles. He knew the deer had yarded here before. After a tough winter you could hardly see the needles for all the poop marbles.

He knelt, and between the trunks he could see them all around him, silent and still save for the puffs of blued fog out their nostrils. Now and then one would flick an ear or stomp a forefoot, still spooked but loath to leave this sheltering space.

Even in the half-light he could see they'd lost the backfat roundness of autumn, the layer that lay beneath the hide and crackled off when he ran them through the skinner. In a corner of the brown pole barn he hadn't bulldozed yet, there was a stack of hay bales he'd failed to feed out before selling the beef cows. Maybe he'd find a way to get them down here. It was odd to see all this life, bedraggled as it was, clustered within sight of his house but shrouded by the boughs. All those hearts chugging in the dark. He felt bad for having spooked them.

He also thought of the echoing freezer. Here were groceries on the hoof. If he shot one, he'd be doing so out of season. Without a license. He'd never violated before. He'd always had a stubborn respect for the law, even when he thought the law was an idiot. But these past few years the deer had proliferated. Holding up traffic in the suburbs, clustering behind the Walmart. There were patches of the country where wolves had whittled them down, but mostly they were every-where. You had to stop for them in the crosswalk in front of McDon-ald's. Hunters were always complaining there weren't enough deer anymore. This from a crowd equipped with elevated and outfitted stands, digital rangefinders, satellite-linked trail cams live-feeding to their cellphones, and piles of bait, legal or otherwise. If not bait, vast soybean or corn fields. The noble hunter, downloading all the help he could get. Most bucks were nicknamed and their racks scored before they got whacked, and it was common practice to order a customized commemorative decal of the antlers in silhouette for placement in the shooter's rear pickup window, in some cases as complement to the nylon bull scrotum dangling from the hitch receiver.

Lately chronic wasting disease was on the rise, but effective interven-tion was blocked by a convergence of commerce, a distrust of govern-ment, general recalcitrance, ham-handed oversight, and interior design predicated on antlers. The bucks got bigger and bigger, less and less venison got eaten, and hunting was on the decline, not so much from antihunters as from all the land bought up by nonhunters who either didn't allow it or leased it to the highest bidder, but the exacerbating factor was the transformation of hunting into yet another over-capi-talized All-American dick-measuring contest, dependent largely on the fragile ego of the pale male. To include himself in the indictment, he still got the shakes when he saw a big rack moving through the tag al-ders and had burned an untold amount of time over the years seeking just that moment. He retained sufficient residual testosterone to feel the elation of killing a monster buck. The sensation was prehistoric and visceral.

He took his first buck at the age of 12 with a bolt-action 30-30 and dumb luck. A spike. Antlers like two Bic pens. But he remembered how his heart hammered. Referring to an old copy of *Sports Afield*, he mounted the skullcap using a piece of pine, some plaster, and brown felt. Returning again to the theme of men and hunting, that wee pair still hung in a corner of the bedroom. In other words, much of what he understood about ego—including everything about it he despised—came from within. Still, he feared the day of the true deerstalker was long gone.

He hauled himself up short. *Feared?* This was definitely *the old days* territory. *Enough of that,* he thought. *Let 'em sort it out on their own.* As if he ever showed up for any of the citizen input meetings. And maybe if he'd been smart enough to lease the hunting rights to this place, he wouldn't be in this particular pickle. In the final analysis, his situation was self-inflicted.

He studied the deer again. It'd be easy enough to take one down in those pines, the herd just standing there. He could take his pick. Try for a doe. Maybe a yearling. Tenderness over trophy, although by now the bucks had shed their antlers.

The shot would be muffled by the snow-cap pines. It'd be a tough drag back, but a tough drag would be right in his wheelhouse. "My whole life has been a…," he began and was immediately cut off by his own internal monologue: *Yeah. We know.*

Once he got the deer home, he'd run it up the skinner he'd built years ago. It was a snatch-block combination of cables and pulleys, a chain and anchor, a modified Vise Grips, and a boat winch. Basically you just cranked the deer out of its skin. Hang the quarters from the barn rafters, slice and freeze the backstraps. Fry up the tenderloins the same night. Drop the medallion in the pan, give it just a kiss of heat, the briefest sear. It took to the tongue like its own pat of butter.

It hungered him to think of it. Then, like a beanbag round to the skull, it hit him: the deer skinner was in the red pole barn. In other words, now buried deep in the ravine.

He was amazed sometimes how deeply he could drift through the cottony meander before barking his shins on reality. Sometimes when he smashed his knuckles, he was surprised to remember he had knuckles.

Chapter Ten

The following morning he took time from the bulldozing to pull the remaining dozen hay bales from the remnants of the brown pole barn. He cleared a spot in the field beside the coop, then pushed the bales there in a pile. By dusk the deer were on it.

Over the next few days, he spent most of the daylight hours on the bulldozer. Early on he deactivated the backup beeper as it triggered his misophonia, and there was no one to back over anyway. He'd reverse at low-idle, enjoying the softer rattle-trap clankety-clank of the tracks. Now and then he'd stop the dozer at a high point, climb atop the hood, and survey the scene. Scraping everything into the ravine was the most definitive thing he'd done in years. He'd run out of fuel before he'd run out of momentum. There was this urge to work, work, work until everything was flat. Everything was smooth. All complications were removed. He was following some duty to clear the earth of unsightly man-made angles.

On a more mundane front, at one point he was chugging along with another piece of the pole barn skidding before his blade when it struck him that this whole exercise would throw the tax assessor for a loop. They were all using satellite imagery these days. Gone were the times when you could tuck a cabin on the back forty undetected. Now you got a laser-printed letter with the deer shack circled and another three or four figures tacked on your bill. He imagined the assessor, his cold coffee and half a doughnut, dutifully scrolling through the electronic plat, maybe tweaking a number here and there, and then the images of his farm sliding into frame, nothing but clear scrapes where all the buildings had been, and the assessor leaning in to stare at the monitor, maybe squinting or scrunching his reading glasses up on his nose, this the most exciting thing he'd seen in weeks, the equivalent of an astronomer spotting a fresh crater on the moon.

He sent another load tumbling into the ravine, spun the dozer 'round, and headed back. The brown pole barn was nearly erased. He knew, of course, that this whole endeavor was an exercise in certifiable nuttiness. That the world would spin on without a wobble. "I can see well enough, without other people telling me, how little all this weighs and is worth and the madness of my design," wrote Montaigne in a quote Harold looked up over lunch.

In high school Harold took that quote to mean, "Aren't I a kook!"

Today he took it with a solid nod.

Later, when the dozer was parked and plugged for the night, he leaned against the blade and thought about JerLuna. He'd begun to construct a narrative around the photograph on the phone, his eavesdropping, and her tears. He had his ideas, but what was the point? He figured heartbreak and betrayal were bitter no matter the variables.

He raised his gaze. Across the fallow land to the far fence line, invisible from here. He flashed to a memory of his father, so far into farming he couldn't back out, standing in this very spot, holding this very gaze, shaking his head and murmuring, "Forty acres deep…"

Chapter Eleven

The next morning when he walked to the coop, it was so cold the trees were popping off like gunshots as the sap locked up. He booted a chunk of snow, and it skittered across the crust, tinkling like a block of balsa wood. Out along the county road, the power lines would be drawn taut and buzzing. All night the house reverberated with the *chonk* of nails retracting within the studs and the click of window glass reframing itself. He didn't need a thermometer to know it was way below zero. He could *hear* it was way below zero. There was no point in starting the dozer today. The diesel would be jelly.

Placing his boot soles in the prints he made the day previous, it occurred to him the impressions were evidence of his past self. Just as quickly he wrinkled his nose and shook his head. *Jejune baloney,* he thought. *Faux-ponderous twaddle. Born of pinheads reading philosophy books.* Which, he realized, leads to knowing the spelling and definition of *jejune* but never being sure how to pronounce it. Not that he'd ever slipped it into conversation down to the feed mill. In the coop he realized he had once again forgotten to bring the egg basket. *But you can spell jejune.*

He packed his pockets.

When he stepped out of the coop, the flat angle of the morning sun threw the surface of the snow into relief, highlighting the dune-like undulations and corrugations, lending it the appearance of an albinic Sahara. Right now everything was still, so *still*. He too stood motionless.

Another tree let out with a crack. This kind of cold was no joke. Stumble into a ravine and break your leg during a heatwave, you might die; stumble into a ravine and break your leg at 30 below, and there was no question.

Down in the draw, a woodpecker rattled. Harold shook his head. It had to be like driving your face into an I-beam hoping for a peanut. Nature was a wonder.

There came a distant airborne roar. It grew, and squinting into the blue, he spotted it: a medevac chopper on a vector to cross his back forty. This was not unusual; his acreage lay below the flight path to a regional trauma center. He studied the hull of the whirlybird, pondered what drama lay cocooned within. Some farmer sucked into a power takeoff shaft, a teenager T-boned in the family minivan, an insurance salesman dying for a cardiac procedure the smaller regional hospital couldn't provide.

He wondered if the pilot could see his bulldozing.

Regardless of what was transpiring up there in the air, it was a reminder that his isolation was an illusion. Stare in motionless silence at a desert of snow, you are still surrounded by a surging, scurrilous world. Back when he was still online and watching the news, it seemed great swathes of the populace had gone all-in for muscle-headed buffoonery egged on by comfy country-clubbers dropping bad-breath platitudes about the ol' ball team. He doubted the republic would recover.

He drew a sliver of hope from a vague sense that the other swathes—those so long shut out and shut down—were studying up behind the scenes. Doing their homework, boning up beyond bumper stickers, doing three times the work just hoping to pull even. *But this is nothing new*, he thought, correcting himself on the fly. Bootstrappy yip-yap abounded, when in fact your average self-proclaimed self-starter got bootstrapped by birthright, and if you traced the tale to its source, you'd find it was often built on the leather of a whip-stroked back. For all the self-sufficiency sermonizing, let the accused dependents put their shoulder in, and suddenly it was an uprising. Among the choice ironies of his life was his observation that your much lauded "salt of the earth" type would in a star-spangled heartbeat salt their fields of freedom rather than cede a square inch to fresh faces and fresh ways.

He wished he could change that. He wished he had more guts, wished he had woke to it all sooner. Wish, wish, wish, whatever. He conjured old Elmer Sorenson, gone now twenty years, down there at the end of the cafe counter: "Country's goin' t'shit, son. Goin' t'shit in a shitwagon."

He thought of his books. All his reading, and what did it bring him. Never mind that, what had it brought him to bring anyone else? Knowledge is power, but what the hell is knowledge in the face of brute force and the thrill of outrage against the weak sauce of your own cowardice? There was a shooting range nearby, and over the course of the last few years, the firing had shifted from carefully spaced marksmanship to rat-a-tat and blammety-blam. He didn't know if this portended revolution or just fun with guns, but either way there had been slippage from the days when the school janitor taught hunter's safety like it was Home Ec as opposed to Call of Duty.

The medevac was receding to invisibility. He wondered if some knucklehead over at the range ever raised his rifle and scoped it across the sky. As the helicopter receded to invisibility, he imagined it descending to a world cacophonous beyond his comprehension. He liked to think he didn't hate people, he hated their noise. That he was misophonic as opposed to misanthropic.

Over the course of this yarny mind meander, his hands had gone numb. He jammed them in his coat pockets, smashing the eggs. *Well hell*, he thought, but was either too cold or too thought-exhausted to flip into his usual rage. Stepping back into the coop he scooped as much of the goop as he could into the feed pans. The chickens swarmed in, gobbling the yolks, the whites, the shells.

Chapter Twelve

The weather moderated, and he worked the dozer steadily. Over the course of a week, he cleared the rest of the brown pole barn, then moved on to the granary and the corn cribs. The milkhouse, the sway-backed machine shed. At one point he bladed up the blown plow truck. Shoved it up the little rise, through the break in the spruce, and right out back. All those years of service, all the hay bales and feed bags hauled and dump runs and country miles with the radio on, even the good early days with her so tight to his side she had to move her knee so he could shift, and yet as it tumbled out of sight he felt nothing.

The thermometer bumped up above freezing for a couple of days, and when he went to collect the eggs, the chicken manure had thawed enough that his breath caught at the ammonia. The chickens didn't seem to care, they just blinked at him like usual, but he still carried enough trace husbandry to feel they deserved better. He created an open space for them outside the door, shoveled down to the earth, and scattered corn to draw them out while he set to with the pitchfork.

Despite all advances, the pitchfork remained the universal sign of farming. He used to pride himself on knowing a pitchfork wasn't just a pitchfork. That there were hay forks and manure forks and potato forks and silage forks, each with its character and ability and distinction. He held a base fascination with the idea that each did a better job—depending on the job—through the simple arrangement of the tines. The hay fork with its three widely spaced tines to pierce and gather the hay in a wad, the broader manure fork with its six tines more narrowly spaced to catch the smaller bits. The silage fork the same but even broader, its tines cupped to form a basket. A farmer south of here had been busted for growing marijuana between rows of field corn. Harold had never tried the stuff, let alone grown it, but idly wondered what kind of fork might be best for handling entire fields of it.

And "pitch." How many decades had he talked about pitching things, even pitching manure, and all those same decades using the term "pitchfork" as simply signifying an object, a fork, of course, but he was well into his forties before the day he saw the verb "pitch" in the compound noun. This wasn't the first time he'd read an old word afresh, and it was always a marvel how a well-read person might go for years without seeing the most obvious meaning a word had to offer.

He paused in his pitching and ran one thumb across the tip of a tine. The steel was worn flat and spatulate, more knife-edge than pencil point. He wondered a moment at how many scoops it had taken to wear away the steel. Where the powdered iron wound up. The idea that there was a weight to everything in the universe. That straw was carbon. That he was carbon. The carbon mice ate the carbon oats and pooped out carbon. And somewhere in the concrete of the barn, of the heifer pens, lay that steel dust. Some of it had been swept outside, some of it flung out the business end of the manure spreader. But it retained its weight in the universe.

He hadn't moved in five minutes. *Holy jeepers*, he thought, jabbing the fork in again, *how useless would I have been if I did smoke weed?*

When he finished spreading fresh straw, the chickens were still enjoying their time in the open air, so he threw them another few handfuls of corn and let them be. No sense trying to chase them back in. Invariably a couple of them would flap out and get stranded in the deep snow, and he'd just wind up chasing them, sweating and cussing. They'd put themselves away at dusk when they returned to roost. He'd close them in then. And he was about out of corn. If he wanted to keep the eggs coming, he'd need to make another trip to town.

He was slow to get going the following day. He lay in bed well past dawn, the light through the curtain crack failing to refresh the stale-aired hole. He felt cradled by inertia, all curled up like a thumbsucker fingering a dirty scrap of blanket. When he was a child, he and his siblings used to fling the door open some winter mornings and run barefooted into the snow, see who could make the longest loop before sprinting back into the house where they'd extend their wet feet to the wood stove and writhe in happy pain as they thawed.

What the hell, he thought, flinging the covers off and thumping down the hall before he had a chance to rethink it. The top step was covered in a fresh few inches, and he hit the yard with a whoop, high-stepping into the deeper stuff wearing nothing but his undies. It was unholy, he supposed, doing such a thing with his dead wife there frozen on the porch, but he was driven partly by madness and partly by memory. And the cold was galvanizing. He hoped it might somehow shake his spirits loose.

He set a goal of the chicken coop and back. Already his toes were going numb, and beneath the new snow the crust scraped his ankles.

But he knew how it would feel fifteen minutes from now, how the cold would shimmer on his skin. He circled around the back of the coop then up past the door.

It was wide open.

Last night, he thought. *I never…*

Chest heaving, he peered inside. The interior was a mess of feathers and blood.

The fisher, he supposed. The fisher, and then when the fisher had its fill and blood was in the air, coyotes. Or a fox. Or a slinking stoat. He looked for tracks, but the fresh snow covered everything. He was dancing in place, his feet beginning to throb. He had to get back to the house before he lost all feeling and broke an ankle. By the time he made it to the porch he had to watch his feet as he placed them, numb as they were. Sitting in the middle of the living room floor, wishing he had stoked the fire first, he clutched his toes and rocked in agony.

An hour later he was bundled up and loading the deer rifle. Without the eggs, with nothing left but feathers, venison had moved up the agenda.

He was barely off the porch when he heard the snowmobiles again. Just across the back valley, on his neighbor's land but obviously having just crossed his. His jaw clenched. The sound of their engines hit him like a dentist's drill.

He raised the rifle. Laid his face against the cheekpiece. Kept both eyes open until he located a snowmobiler in the scope. Closed his left eye and swung the crosshairs past the man's helmet, past the weasel-skull cowling, out front a few feet and then aimed about a foot high. He was flat-out spit-balling on the windage, although he figured he was close on the range. When he was a boy his mother let him check out the local library's copy of the *Shooter's Bible Guide to Ballistics* so he could study up on the firearms name-checked in the cowboy books he read. Thus, he retained a modest working knowledge of how much altitude his bullet would lose crossing the distance between the muzzle and yonder sledding jackasses. Those paperback cowboys favored Winchesters and the Sharps .50 "buffler" guns. His was a run-of-the-mill bolt-action 30-06 with a fiberglass stock, but then he'd never felt much like a cowboy anyway. He did remember reading in a Louis L'Amour book that you had to aim high when shooting downhill to allow for the effects of gravity. No, wait, shoot *low*. Never mind, those snowmobilers were across the valley but pretty much on the level with him. He squeezed the trigger, and the rifle jumped. It was good to feel the kick of it against his shoulder. The liveliness of it. A solid smack, a reminder he was flesh and bone.

The snow spray leapt betwixt the first and second snowmobile. *Hoo*, he thought. Helmeted and swaddled in gear, knee-clamping their screaming machines, not one of the sled jockeys noticed. He jacked out the empty and racked a second, then hung the gun in the crook of his arm and just stood there. The snowmobiles were already receding, crossing just below the hill crest, then up and over, smooth as you please. He envisioned the riders later, their suits unzipped to their waists, guffawing over longnecks at the next tavern stop, utterly unaware of the bullet. *The unexamined life*, he thought, *or some sort of metaphorical corollary*. Then, *Perhaps I should have been a professor.*

The meetings and politics would have killed him, but the vocabulary woulda been a hoot.

He caught a whiff of the burnt powder and pressed the heel of his free hand against the chamber, felt the residual warmth, and recalled how his father taught him to shoot. He was nine years old, and his father's voice was low and steady as he set tin cans on a log. There was nothing gun-slingy about it. It occurred to him that he had just now fired a shot in anger. A clean miss, but suddenly the phrase had weight.

He unloaded and returned the rifle to the house. He could no longer imagine shooting a deer. He supposed he should have felt jitters, or relief. Catharsis. Rather he felt pleased for having indulged the moment. Not exultant, not celebratory, just satisfied to have for once done what he felt. It startled him to realize if he'd managed to put a bullet through that dude's helmet, he'd have reacted no less calmly.

Chapter Thirteen

All the bulldozing, and he had recovered his deftness with the blade. Compared to all the other demolition he'd done, sweeping the chicken coop into the ravine was as easy as nudging a jewelry box across a marble counter. As it tipped and crashed from sight, he spun the dozer and looked things over. Only two structures left: the garage and the house.

He rattled up to the garage and stopped. Studied it. It was countersunk into the hill, so there'd be some earthmoving. He stared a bit longer. Then he jammed the throttle forward, but rather than plowing into the building he diverted out the driveway.

He plowed out to the county road and back, then cleared the space before the garage door and started her car.

In town, his first stop was at the attorney's office. He had this half-baked idea of how he might keep the human vultures from his land. It was awkward at first, him in their carpeted reception area looking like a wind-burned Sasquatch and with no appointment, but they slotted him in, albeit in the backmost conference room and with a general sense of caution. He unfolded the online will he and his wife had printed out but never completed and smoothed it against the long, clean table.

An hour later he drove slowly past the coffee shop. The boy with the curly hair was at a window seat, coloring. He could see JerLuna behind the bar, working the espresso machine. He kept moving, although he knew she wouldn't recognize his wife's car. He spotted JerLuna's vehicle and pulled in beside it. She was still riding the miniature spare. Checking to be sure this segment of the lot wasn't visible from the shop, he sprung the trunk of his wife's car, producing a lug wrench and the hydraulic jack that had leaked on his kitchen table. All his shop supplies being in the ravine, he'd dug around in the pantry and filled the jack reservoir with vegetable oil. It made a squish noise and bubbled around the seal as he pumped, but it lifted and held as he switched the mini spare for the full-size spare he'd always insisted his wife carry.

After a final check to be sure the lug nuts were tight, he leaned the mini-spare against the driver's side door so JerLuna would find it, and then he drove off. The coffee shop was near the university campus, and he could see the antenna of the college radio station, so he tuned it in. It felt odd to hear that music in the car and not the truck. The student host was awkward but sincere. "That was a little Lucinda Williams," she said. "And now a little Jimmy LaFave." The song opened like a slow afternoon in a wide open space, and although the host hadn't said so, he figured based on the chorus the title was "Going Home." By the second verse he had to pull off the road, the tears were coming that hard.

It took three more songs and a series of outdated public service announcements, but he got it back together and drove on. He had forgotten McGruff the Crime Dog even existed.

Chapter Fourteen

Once home, he pulled the car inside, then rolled down and latched the garage door. Then he started the bulldozer. The fuel gauge needle was resting solidly on the peg below the "E." He navigated at an idle out toward the ravine. At one point he turned halfway 'round in his seat and surveyed the scene behind him. White, white. Clean and white. The farmhouse, the countersunk garage, and nothing else.

At the precipice of the ravine he stopped, opened the seat-side toolbox, and pulled out a bungee cord. Tapping the throttle up just a touch, he lassoed the steer levers with the bungee, snaked it through the guard bar, looped it back, and re-hooked it to the steer levers. The dozer nosed forward, and he jumped clear.

The machine chugged ahead, tipped forward, and disappeared. There was the sound of cracking brush, a modulation when the exhaust pipe snapped, then just the engine idling roughly and clank of the track pads rotating. He peeked over the edge. It had landed belly-up. A curl of white smoke showed—leaking oil, he supposed—but nothing dramatic. He turned for the house and made it maybe ten yards before the engine died, and that was that.

Back in the house, he decided he'd try drinking. Just this once. Erase his mind for an evening. In the kitchen he reached into the pantry and felt around the top shelf until he found the gin bottle. Took it into the bedroom, lay down atop the unmade mess.

She was never much of a drinker, but she'd ask for a gin and tonic now and again. In the early days, he would mix one and bring it to her, the ice clinking, the glass sweat cool on his fingertips as he handed her the tumbler. "Thank you honey," she would say, tipping her head back for a kiss. He stared at the ceiling and held the image in his head; the angle of her neck, the tumbler held away to one side, her free hand touching his shoulder, her eyes…

He couldn't see them.

Hoarfrost sprung up in his guts: here was his irretrievable sin.

He had rendered her faceless.

There was no forgiveness for this. There was no living with it. Philosophication did nothing but reverse engineer the rot. He had ceased to see her for who she was. Had stopped *searching* for who she was. *When was the last time,* he wondered, *he had looked her in the eyes he could no longer conjure?*

He looked at the bedroom walls, thought of the barn before it burned, the cows in their stanchions, the mow packed with hay, him walking to the house after chores, her at the sink, leaning into the roundness of the baby in her belly. Under certain conditions in winter, when the air is dry, snow evaporates without turning to water. Sublimation, they called it. Nothing to see, no trickling melt, just a shrinking and settling, snow transforming invisibly to air.

In the living room, he knelt and stoked the fire. Pine strips and oak so dry it struck the grates with a xylophone clink. He closed and latched the glazed door. Set the draft wide open, watched the flames ribbon and rise. As the blaze gained, he laid a nest of kindling on the carpet. Now the stove trembled with combustion. Taking the ash rake in hand, he opened the door and drew a clutch of coals across the carpet and kindling. Smoke spun to the ceiling and gathered. The kindling caught.

He went to the porch, unwrapped her body and moved it just inside the front door. Next he retrieved the box of photos. He pulled the Polaroid of the baby and placed it on her chest. Then he placed the box beside the fire growing on the living room carpet.

He retrieved the gin bottle and her sleeping pills from the bedroom. Took them to the kitchen. Sweeping his forearm across the table to clear a space, he drew out a chair and sat. Uncapping the pill bottle, he tipped it back like a shot glass, then chased it with a slug of gin. He gasped, and his eyes watered. But he kept the pace: pills, swig, pills, swig. He could hear a faint crackling from the living room. His back was to the flames, but the light of them was shuddering across the kitchen wall. Once again he thought of the burning barn. When there was no more rattle in the pill bottle, he pitched it over his shoulder into the fire.

Back in the bedroom he lay in the blankets and pulled at the last of the gin. From his time with the fire department, he knew how they'd read it: standard wood stove mishap. *Homeowner stoked fire before retiring for the evening, failed to latch door, sparks ignited carpet and spread. Male remains discovered in bedroom area. Empty bottle indicates decedent may have been intoxicated, toxicology tests pending. Female remains found near front door, likely overcome while attempting to escape.*

The bulldozing would not be so simply explained.

She, on the other hand, would have cut to the heart of it. *You didn't want to deal with it, so you pushed it all away. You couldn't fix it, so you burned it down.* He still couldn't see her face, but he heard her voice, clear as day.

Things were slipping sideways. He rose and put a hand out to steady himself against the wall. Reached out with his other and turned the snapshot of them smiling in the barn face down on the dresser. *Lest she return in the form of a ghost,* he thought, through his thickening fog; he had left her so long ago she should not have to see the image of him beside her. He half pulled his clothes off, fell back on the bed, and drew the covers to his chin. By the time the smoke layered itself downward to his face, he was sleeping and breathed it easily in.

Chapter Fifteen

The envelope arrived at the coffee shop amongst all the other mail. It was late afternoon before she got to it. Enclosed was a letter enfolding a business card.

I stumbled into that coffee shop like a rube and you were kind to me. There's not enough of that.

The business card is a lawyer. Call him. He will explain everything. It's written up pretty bullet-proof. Lawyers are merciless which is why merciful people need them.

Turns out because I inherited the farm from my father, the state viewed it as my individual property. I never thought of it that way. She gave as much as I did. More. But she's gone. And the law allows me to do this legally and cleanly. So I will. There's no one else to claim it anyways.

I left you her car too. In the garage. It should start. We never missed an oil change. Tires are good. Needs a spare.

I shouldn't say this but I feel a need to. She died a while back. Nothing evil. She just passed in the night. I could look you in the eyes and tell you that. We'd been hiding so long after losing the baby, I didn't want anyone out here asking questions. Then I waited so long there was no way to explain my waiting. You and the lawyer are the only ones who know this. Her dying first made it legal for me to write this will. Like I said, bullet-proof.

There's no money left. Just the land. Sell it all. Or keep a little patch for yourself. Do what's best for you and your little one. There's an orthopedic surgeon who's been drooling over the backmost 80 ever since he moved in. He's got what my dad used to call "the gotta-have-its." Got it bad. Charge him up the ying-yang. The lawyer can put you in touch.

This is not a rescue. This doesn't fix my fuckups. This is paying privilege forward. I read about it on your bulletin board.

I took that bulldozer and I cleaned everything up. You won't have to deal with my crap. I don't know if we live beyond this earth, but if we do I hope atonement is part of the deal.

I did it this way because there is no need for me anymore. But there is great need for you. For your child. For I guess what I'd call fresh hearts.

Do better than I did.
Good luck.

Harold

P.S. Your tip.

She checked the envelope again. A twenty-dollar bill.

Epilogue

The snow fell and fell, covering the earthen bald spot where the chicken coop had been scraped clear, laying a ribbed mallow-top over the dozer tracks. The yellow caution tape crackled in the cold wind, the remains of the house a strewn hump after the fire department pulled it apart and drowned the coals. All around, the land lay white. In time, the first green shoot cracked the earth, opened its cotyledon arms, and gathered in the sun. There followed soon the laughter of a curly-haired child echoing joyfully from a ravine, where at dusk he emerged dirty and happy, hatchet in hand.

Acknowledgments

First and foremost, my parents—anything decent is because of them, anything else is simply not their fault. Brittany Olson for the first read and deepest encouragement. William Thedinga, Jerrika Mighelle, and Joy Kirkpatrick for their time and guidance. Tricia Duyfhuizen for giving it shape and style, RT Vrieze for the cover art.

Ben Shaw for things between and beyond.

My wife and daughters, watching me shovel in circles.

Musical influences:
Sound & Fury by Sturgill Simpson
"Hard on Everyone" from *Total Freedom* by Kathleen Edwards
Break Me Open by S. Carey
Stasis Sounds for Long-Distance Space Travel by 36 & zakè

About the Author

Michael Perry was raised on a small dairy farm.
He lives online at SneezingCow.com.

Where to Get Help

Don't go down alone. If you are suicidal, call 911, your local emergency services, or the National Suicide Prevention Lifeline 24/7 at 988 or 1-800-273-8255 or text HELLO to 741741. All contact is confidential.

Agricultural professions have among the highest suicide rates. More and more people are recognizing this, more and more people are stepping up to help, and more and more people are reaching out for help. If you're a farmer or live in a rural area, consider the following resources:

National Agricultural Law Center map linking to hotlines by state: https://nationalaglawcenter.org/center-publications/family/mental-health/

National Suicide Prevention Lifeline: 988 or 1-800-273-8255 or text the Crisis Text Line (text HELLO to 741741). Both services are free and available twenty-four hours a day, seven days a week.

Social media, for all its deranged darkness, can also be a source of light and connection. Twitter's @domoreag and @AgMentalHealth are two examples. In my home state, ruralwomensinitiative.org is another.

Your state department of agriculture and local extension offices will have even more regionally specific sources of mental health assistance.

Your pastor, your family, your knucklehead pal…tell someone.

Please don't try to plow it under.

www.ingramcontent.com/pod-product-compliance
Lightning Source LLC
Chambersburg PA
CBHW031544310726
48971CB00008B/2620